I slipped the safety, took a long breath, held it, and put the crosshairs in the right place. I took up the slack in that damn military trigger and began to squeeze off. Then the gun fired.

The recoil came back at me with authority, throwing the scope up off the target; the room shook with the blast of the .30 caliber cartridge. Even as I brought the scope back down, Governor Martin Maney—the man I'd just fired at—was still standing there. Then suddenly, after all the noise and fuss had died down, he spun around and fell on the sidewalk. I saw the bullet make a splash against the Bank, having passed clear through.

That's when the door swung open and I turned around and saw the girl, her voice faintly puzzled, saying, "What's going on in here, anyway? What was that awful noise?"

IN THE GREAT TRADITION OF THE MATT HELM SERIES COMES A NOVEL OF BREATH-TAKING INTRIGUE BY
DONALD HAMILTON

LINE OF FIRE

by Donald Hamilton

A Gold Medal Book

GOLD MEDAL BOOKS
Fawcett Publications, Inc., Greenwich, Conn.
Member of American Book Publishers Council, Inc.

I HAD WORKED out the range from the window to the yellow fire hydrant down at the intersection three blocks away. It was four hundred and twenty-six yards on a scale map of the city; four hundred and twenty-two by counting paces and calculating angles. The difference wasn't enough to worry about. I had a sandbag rest for the gun just inside the window and a six-power telescopic sight. The gun itself was a star-gauge Springfield they had picked up for me; it would shoot better than inch groups at a hundred yards now that I had tuned it and learned what ammunition it liked. Most people don't seem to know it, but guns are very particular about what you feed them; what'll shoot like a dream through one musket will spray all over the landscape from another. This particular gas pipe liked the hundred-and-eighty-grain bullet in front of a hot load of forty-seven and a half grains of Hi Vel No. 2 powder which pushed it along, I figured, at better than twenty-eight hundred feet per second.

At a quarter of three I eased the window open. The day was fine for the job. There was an overcast that might have made trouble if I'd had to judge the range; it's hard to estimate distance accurately on a cloudy day. Since I knew the distance already, this did not matter. What was important was that there wasn't a breath of wind. I had told them that if there was more than a five-mile breeze the deal was off for the day. I wasn't going to do any fancy four-hundred-yard shooting with a wind blowing—not in a city street where it'll change directions six times a minute.

The jerk they had put in there with me was chain smoking by this time. He kept offering me cigarettes, but I don't smoke when I have shooting to do. A little target practice before and after will teach you the difference—about ten points in the score. At ten minutes of three I got the gun lined up, sitting beside the table, bench-rest fashion. The big scope picked out the yellow hydrant clear and bright. The

5

jerk—his name was Sam something-or-other, but they all called him Whitey—was shooting his cuff every fifteen seconds to look at his watch.

"It'd be just like the little bastard to be late," he said.

I didn't say anything to this. There's a certain kind of person who makes a point of believing that it always rains on his picnics and nobody else's. At five minutes of three I got the shells out and pressed four of them down into the magazine, slid the fifth into the chamber, closed the bolt, and set the safety.

The jerk lit another cigarette, looked at his watch, and peered out the window. He was an undersized, overdressed character with bad teeth. He took out an automatic pistol and fiddled with it; it was a P-38, brought back by some GI, I suppose; not the rough model the Germans were slapping together toward the end of the war, or one of those booby-trap guns assembled afterward, from the parts left over at the factory, to be traded for American cigarettes. This was an early version, and a pretty good gun.

I said, "Put that thing away."

"Listen—"

I flicked the safety of the Springfield and slid the bolt open and started to unload, rising. He brandished his war souvenir.

"Where the hell do you think you're going?"

"Home," I said. "Unless you get that damn thing out of sight."

"Listen—"

"Listen yourself," I said. "I don't like people playing with loaded firearms in the same room with me. It makes me nervous. When I'm nervous I can't shoot straight. Put it away and keep your hand off it or the whole deal's off."

He said, "Well, if you're scared of it—"

I said, "Anybody who isn't scared of a loaded gun is a damn fool."

"Listen—"

"It's two minutes of three," I said. "Make up your mind. One way or the other."

"Ah, hell—" After a moment he put the gun back under his armpit. "You'd better make this damn good, is all I have to say," he said.

I said, "Just sit down somewhere and stop bothering me and I'll make it good."

I closed the bolt again, settled myself with the gun, and picked up the hydrant in the scope; then swung the gun back and forth through a few degrees to examine the possible field of fire. It was a good enough place. I had picked it myself. The avenue below me ended at the cross street down there, so that I was shooting into the blank stone wall of the County Bank, against which the bullet could be counted on to disintegrate. Somebody might be scratched by a piece of stone or flying metal, but there wouldn't be any ricochets whining around to kill innocent bystanders.

A woman walked through the field of the scope, letting the crosshairs pass right over her. It gave me a funny feeling, and I raised the gun a trifle so that it would not be aimed directly at the pedestrians over there. You get a nasty sense of power when you look at someone over the sights of a loaded gun: a few ounces of pressure on the trigger and they're dead, and it's all up to you.

Then the jerk, who had picked up the binoculars, hissed at me; and a moment later Maney walked into the field of the scope with another man I did not recognize. Maney's small, square figure was unmistakable, however; the scope pulled him right into the room. I saw him stop by the hydrant to make some point in the argument he was having with the other man. He'd been to the eye-doctor that morning, and the dark glasses he was wearing now gave his face a blind and blank look, even at that distance.

The jerk was hissing at me to make it snappy now. I slipped the safety again, took a long breath, held it, and put the crosshairs in the right place. I took up the slack in that damn military trigger and began to squeeze off. The trick is not to know when the piece is going to fire; that is, your brain knows, but your finger can't be let into the secret or it'll yank and throw the shot off.... At the last instant, Maney clinched his argument with that famous gesture of his of throwing his hand up into the air as if grabbing for something. Then the gun fired.

Four hundred yards is a long way, even for a bullet traveling better than twice the speed of sound. The gun came back at me with authority, throwing the scope up off the target; the room shook with the blast of the .30-caliber cartridge. All this happened, and I brought the scope back down, and Maney was still standing there. Then, suddenly, after all the noise and fuss had died down, he spun around and fell on the sidewalk. I saw the bullet make a splash against the Bank, having passed clear through. Well, I thought, you've done it now, boy!

"You hit him!" the jerk cried. *"You hit him. He's down!"*

He dropped the binoculars and swung to face me. I got up from my chair. The door opened, and a girl's voice said, faintly puzzled, "What's going on in here, anyway? What was that awful noise?"

chapter two

THERE WASN'T, of course, supposed to be anybody up here on the third floor on a Saturday afternoon; this had been checked and double-checked. In fact, I had made sure of the neighboring offices myself before coming in here today. One belonged to an insurance outfit and the other to some kind of mail-order business and both were closed for the week-end. Furthermore, the door was supposed to be locked, but a combination of nerves, too much whisky the night before and a weak bladder, had made it necessary for the jerk to pay a visit down the hall. Apparently he had forgotten to slip the latch on his return.

Anyway, there she stood in the doorway, a slightly built girl of medium height, wearing glasses, looking crisp and fresh and cool in a summer suit of that striped blue-and-white cord material that's also used for men's lightweight suits. A little round hat of the same material was pulled down on her dark hair. She was wearing white gloves, nylons, and blue-and-white pumps. She was carrying a white purse and several packages—enough that she had her hands full and had to take a fresh grip on the load now that she had. got the door open.

Then Whitey had her inside. The packages spilled to the floor; he had to kick one out of the way to close the door again. The girl opened her mouth to protest indignantly, and he gave her a backhanded slap across the face that knocked her glasses off and slammed her back against the wall so hard that she lost her grip on the purse. She crouched there, gasping. I had time for a sense of impending doom, so to speak. The operation had already gone sour, but now it was curdled like last week's milk in August. Whitey's hand had already started its familiar journey toward his armpit.

"Whitey!" I said, but the jerk was on his way, at last. He had been cocked and ready all day. There was no stopping him now. The situation had a nice nightmare quality, one thing leading smoothly into another: it was like going to hell on roller skates. I saw the liberated P-38 come out. The Germans did a good design job on that gun; it's the only automatic pistol in the world, so far as I know, that can be carried with the hammer down, safe as a slab of cheese, and still be fired, through a double-action mechanism, with a simple pull on the trigger. Whitey was pulling even as the gun came clear of his coat. The girl by the wall just stared, petrified. She was just a kid, I saw, and her eyes had a weak and innocent look without the glasses. Everything seemed to be happening in a kind of ruthless slow motion.

I suppose I could have hit him with something; maybe I could have reasoned with him. That's the trouble with having firearms around; they supply a simple and drastic answer to almost every problem. I won't say that the fact that I was already pretty fed up with the bastard didn't have something to do with what happened next. The heavy Springfield was swinging around before the conscious thought was in my mind. The gun was a part of me; I had lived with it for weeks, preparing for the job. I wasn't even aware of working the bolt to eject the fired shell. There wasn't time to get the butt to my shoulder; there was just time to turn and fire. At that range it made no difference at all.

The gun leaped backward in my hands. The bullet took Whitey just below the armpit with some twenty-eight hundred foot seconds of velocity and just about three thousand foot pounds of energy. A man shot with a high-powered rifle at close range doesn't just die, he kind of comes apart at the seams. Whitey ceased to exist, as Whitey, when the .30-caliber slug hit him. He was dead long before he reached the floor, and there was stuff on the wall beyond him. The room was rocking with the muzzle blast; plaster trickled from the ceiling. I kept track of that damn P-38 although there was nothing I could do to stop it from going off if it wanted to; however, it hit the floor harmlessly and skittered back into a corner.

The girl put her hands flat against her mouth and pressed hard as if to stuff the screams back inside, as she stared at the body on the floor. I guess she had never seen a dead man except on TV. But Whitey wasn't acting and it wasn't ketchup. I looked at the gun in my hands. Well, I could hardly blame it on the gun. There were sirens down the street now; that would be the police, and the ambulance for Maney. It was time to go. I laid the Springfield into the long, black, leather-covered case. I don't know if they make trombones forty-six inches long; the point is, most other people don't know either. I dropped in the two boxes of cartridges I had taken out. I found the ejected shell and dropped that in. There was room for the binoculars, too. I closed the case.

The kid was still plastered against the wall in the same place. Her hands were now pressed flat against the wall on either side of her, holding her up; in spite of this she seemed to have slid down a little, bunching up her jacket in back. She looked kind of as if somebody had hung her there on a hook, by the collar.

Everything was quite clear in my mind; I could see how they would work this out, and it would work out beautifully. Whitey, dead, would be put to good use. You could almost say that I had done them a favor; this was going to be a much better-looking setup than the original plan. However, I wasn't counting on gratitude or appreciation, either for me or the girl in front of me, who had been a contributing factor. It was obvious that I couldn't leave her. I might as well have let Whitey shoot her. She had seen too much.

I found her glasses, unbroken, and set them on her nose. I put her purse in her hands, and the packages, and she took them numbly. I picked up the trombone case, remembered the P-38, picked that up and stuck it in my belt, and turned back to take the kid by the arm. She cringed away from me. The fact that I had saved her from Whitey hadn't registered. There had been two nasty men with guns and one had shot the other. There had been noise and smoke and blood and violence. She was, quite naturally, shocked and scared beyond thinking or reasoning. At the moment, the only difference between Whitey and me, in her mind, was that Whitey was dead. She might have been right, at that.

"Snap out of it," I said. "Just behave yourself and you'll be all right."

She licked her lips and straightened up. She seemed startled to learn that she could stand on her feet without a wall to hold her up. She moved with me to the door, clumsily, like somebody learning to walk again after a long illness. A siren whined down the avenue outside. The police were working fast. They would have to; their jobs were at stake. This wasn't an ordinary shooting. This was Maney. I turned left in the hall, away from the stairs and toward the fire escape.

"Have you got a car?" I asked the kid. It seemed probable that they would be on the getaway car in a few minutes; every prowl car in the city would undoubtedly have the number and description in the time it took one of the boys to learn what had happened and get on the phone. I didn't think they would hesitate for a minute over turning me in; they had never really trusted me. The kid did not answer my question. I stopped and shook her sharply. Her hat fell off. "A car," I snapped. "Have you—"

"Y-Yes."

"Where?"

"—parking lot." It was kind of a gasp.

"Where?"

"B-Behind—behind O'Hearn's."

I picked up the hat and crammed it back on her head. Burdened with the gun, I had to release her to do it, and she made a belated, half-hearted move to run, but I grabbed her again and marched her down the empty hall. More sirens went by outside.

I said, "I've just finished saving your life once and I'm trying to save it again. Don't make it too hard for me. I discourage easily."

There was no sign that I had impressed her in any way. She stumbled along beside me, dragging a little. At the window at the end of the hall I set the gun case down and, left-handed, threw the latch off and got the sash open. She started out obediently, but her narrow skirt gave her some difficulty; she had to pause to take a reef in it before she could get her leg over. I went out after her, still holding her, retrieved the gun, got the window down so as not to leave too obvious a trail; then we were running down the iron stairs making a hell of a racket. Fortunately there was no one in the alley. The swinging, counterweighted lowest section sank under our weight and rose up again behind us.

I stopped the kid before we reached the street. She leaned against the brick wall of the building, catching her breath. She looked like something dumped out of a laundry basket; she looked like a tough day and a hard night instead of only about five minutes of terror.

"Pull yourself together," I said. "Your slip is showing." She made some mechanical gestures. "That's better," I said. "Now fix your hair and get your hat straight." She went through the motions. The results were surprisingly good; it's something they can do in their sleep, I guess. "Okay," I said. "Now let's see you smile. Walk along beside me and remember this isn't a water pistol I've got here. . . ."

We reached the avenue and took the sidewalk to the left; a young man—well, thirty isn't ancient—with a musical instrument of some kind, and a young lady with the fruits of an afternoon's shopping. A prowl car went by, hitting the siren lightly from time to time, just enough to make it growl. I didn't look at it. Some of the men on the force knew me from the shop.

"I tell you," I said, "it was a scream, darling. You should have been there. Larry was tanked to the tonsils and making passes at every female in sight. He's a card, Larry is. Funniest man I know. It's too bad he had to fall off the chandelier and fracture a vertebra. They say he'll be in a cast for months."

It was five blocks up the avenue to O'Hearn's department store. They had never seemed quite so long. The municipal parking lot behind it was crowded. The girl guided me along the rows of diagonally parked cars to a '62 Chevy convertible in a back corner. We had timed it just right; the red violation flag was just about to pop up. A minute more and the kid would have been liable to a dollar fine. She stopped and looked at me questioningly. The walk had steadied her. There was intelligence in her eyes; and contempt for me and everything I stood for, not that she knew what that was, but she was doing some fancy guessing.

"Okay," I said. "The key. You drive."

She shuffled her bundles and brought the purse to the top. A siren came wailing down the avenue, moving fast. The sound trailed off abruptly as the prowl car stopped about five blocks back the way we had come. Another joined it.

I glanced at my watch. Eight minutes past three. The lads in blue were right on schedule; apparently knowledge of the changed situation had not yet percolated through official channels.

The girl was listening, too. She glanced at me, and made a quick movement. All the bundles flew out of her arms; and the white purse spun away from her and slid under the next car. The kid squared her shoulders and faced me heroically, waiting for the bullet. She was helping the police; she had done her best to delay me; now she was prepared to die.

I grinned at her and took out the P-38. "Go get it," I said.

"What?" She looked shocked.

"Crawl under and get it."

"I won't. You don't dare shoot. The noise would bring the police."

I said, "Go get it, sister."

I pulled the hammer back to cock. I didn't need to, but it made an impressive little click. The girl's eyes wavered. Logic should have told her that I hadn't saved her from Whitey just to have the pleasure of blowing holes in her myself, but logic, either mine or hers, didn't look very convincing to her at the moment. A couple walked past, laden with packages. I turned so that the gun was hidden from them. They paid no attention to us. There seemed to be sirens wailing all over town. I couldn't see much hope in the situation, but then, there hadn't been much hope in my situation for quite a while—two and a half years, to be exact. I had nothing to lose by playing the hand out; and the kid had her life to gain. There was a kind of perverse satisfaction in trying to save her despite herself; it wouldn't have been half as much fun if she had believed in me and trusted me. A man in my shoes takes his fun where he finds it. I found pleasure in the fact that she, noble and self-sacrificing, was slitting her own throat, and not in the way she thought, either; while I, a sadistic bully, was saving her life.

"Get down and get it," I said harshly.

She remembered how Whitey had looked when the bullet hit him; she got down and tried to reach under while sitting on her heels. She looked up at me helplessly. I moved the gun slightly, and let it come steady, sighting. She licked her lips, drew up her skirt, and got down on her knees; then abruptly, with a little gasp, threw herself on the ground and wiggled forward, got the purse, and squirmed back out again. I took the purse from her. She got up and started to brush herself off but checked herself, seeing the dirt on her gloves.

"All right," I said, unlocking the car. "Now get in and drive and behave yourself." I laid the case with the Springfield in the back and heaved her packages after it. I got in beside her. "Out Lincoln Avenue to Western," I said. "Stay on Western until I tell you. Don't break any laws. Don't wink at any policemen. Let's go."

chapter three

THE CUTOFF brought us out on No. 401 just below Annandale. We drove west from there about ten miles, came north on the little road they tell me used to be an extension of the Capital City trolley line—in the days when you could take a streetcar anywhere—and headed east on U.S. 54 which took us back into the city, through the commercial south side with the factories and filling stations and tourist courts. Nobody showed any interest in us. I had the kid turn south again on Division Street. We followed that out until it became a little country road that ducked under the new turnpike; a couple of miles farther on we turned east again. I know that area better than most people, in spite of having lived there only a couple of years. You get to know a country when you drive around it with a gun after quail, squirrel, and rabbits in season; crows and woodchucks the rest of the year. When we hit the Poplar Island road I had the kid turn south and keep going, figuring that would be the last route they'd expect me to take.

Presently I lifted the trombone case into the front seat. The original plan had been to leave the Springfield in that third floor room. It was supposed to be traced to a little rat named Tony something-or-other who, if the plans hadn't been canceled in time, would be on his way to Mexico by now, leaving a clear trail behind him, at least for a distance.

He had a motive of sorts; Maney had refused a pardon to his brother as a result of which the brother had recently passed away in the death cell of the state prison. Tony was being well paid for his vacation. I understood that he had been quite willing to do the shooting for a slight additional fee; he had been turned down on the grounds that he couldn't shoot well enough. None of those pool-hall characters can hit a house at fifty yards.

I opened the case and lifted the gun out. I'm a little nuts about guns, I suppose; to me there's nothing more beautiful in the world, and I don't mean your bird's-eye maple stocks and fancy engraving. I mean the gun itself: the way the barrel fits into the wood of the fore end; the way the bolt slides in the polished steel of the action; the way. . . . Well, to hell with that schmalz. Anyway, I was glad I hadn't left my baby behind to gather rust and dust as Exhibit A.

The kid squirmed slightly beside me; I realized that she had been watching out of the corner of her eye as I ran my hand along the smooth walnut stock. She probably thought I was congratulating myself on what I had done to Whitey, and maybe drooling a little in anticipation of what I was going to do to her. I unloaded the gun, which was what I had brought it out for. Habit is a funny thing. I'd had good training where firearms were concerned; and I couldn't be comfortable knowing that I had put a weapon away with shells in the magazine. I wiped off the metal parts with an oily rag, closed the case, and laid it in back again.

A state police car passed us in the other lane. The boys in the big hats paid us no attention. I watched the kid's face tighten as they drove past; her gloved hands squeezed the steering wheel; but she couldn't quite bring herself to do it. Then they were gone, and her face relaxed, and her eyes got a little wet behind the glasses—with disappointment, I suppose, and frustration, and disgust with herself for not having had the nerve to yell something while there was a chance. She was quite a pretty girl, I noticed, despite the glasses. I judged her age to be twenty-two or three; but I could have been a couple of years off either way. Most of the time she looked like a kid—under the abnormal conditions under which I had observed her, at least—but sometimes she had an odd little air of maturity.

I watched her settle herself more comfortably behind the wheel. The police car had been her last hope, I guess; now she was resigning herself to sticking around for a while. Presently she slowed the car so that she could strip off her soiled gloves. She dropped them on the seat between us with a look of distaste, and brushed off the front of her jacket, and pulled her skirt down more tidily, and brushed at it. She was making herself at home, getting set for the long haul, realizing that rescue wouldn't be as quick and easy as she had let herself hope. When she gripped the wheel again, bare handed, I noticed the rings. It always makes a little difference to know they're married; although I don't know why it should have, under the circumstances.

I filled my pipe and lighted it. "What the hell were you doing in the building, anyway?" I asked.

She didn't answer at once. Then she said, "Why, I—" and hesitated, and colored slightly. "I just had to— Well, I work there."

"Where?"

"North Star Insurance. I'm Mr. Fenwick's secretary."

"Who's Mr. Fenwick?"

"He's North Star Insurance."

"Okay," I said. "Go on."

"Well, I work there," she said. "And naturally I've got a key to the.... I mean, I haven't been in the city long, and the only place I knew was in O'Hearn's, and I didn't want to have to walk all the way back there when I hadn't finished looking at dresses.... " Her voice trailed away.

I said, "You were just up there to use the john, is that it?"

"Y-Yes."

"You have a key to it, and the building was open...." I burst out laughing. She squirmed and looked at me resentfully.

"It isn't *that* funny!"

"You wouldn't understand," I said. "Here's the whole damn state in an uproar, and why? Just because two damn fools couldn't hold their water. If you hadn't had to go, you wouldn't have been there; and if Whitey hadn't had to go, he wouldn't have left our door unlocked so that you could stick your nose in.... Kid, what's the matter with you, anyway?"

"What do you mean?"

"Didn't your mother ever tell you it was rude to be inquisitive about guns going off? People resent it. Why the hell didn't you take off down the stairs and grab the nearest policeman, if you simply had to be public-spirited?"

She said, a little angrily, "I didn't know it *was* a sh It sounded like an explosion."

I said, "Honey, explosions like to be left alone. They're sensitive about privacy. . . . What's the matter?"

She was rubbing her ears, first one and then the other, as if the conversation had reminded her of something that had been bothering her.

"They hurt," she said.

"You stood almost in front of a .30-06 when it went off. You'll know it for a couple of days." I remembered something, too, and pulled the cotton out of my ears and tossed it out the car window. If the police could make something of a couple of wads of cotton by the roadside, they were welcome to it. I glanced at my hands, but didn't take off the thin pigskin gloves I was wearing, as I had to decide what I was going to do about the kid and her car before I started leaving fingerprints around. I said, conversationally, "Did you ever see a movie called *Shane?* It's the only time Hollywood ever managed to make gunfire sound like the real thing. Usually it sounds like popcorn in a skillet."

She looked at me in a funny, wary way. "Tell me something," she said, and hesitated, not knowing, obviously, whether she dared to gamble on my reactions. She screwed up her courage and came out with it: "Tell me something; are you crazy?"

I grinned, and saw the relief that came into her eyes; she had taken a long chance with that one, or thought she had.

I said, "It's a good question. What do you think?"

She hesitated again. I could see the way her mind was working; if she could keep me talking on this personal—even intimate—level, she might be able to gain my confidence; perhaps she could even persuade me to let her go. On the other hand, I was obviously an unstable character, and might object violently to too much familiarity—or, worse, might even get a notion to take advantage of it. She certainly didn't want to put any ideas into my head. It was a neat balancing act she had to perform; but then she was—or thought she was—fighting for her life.

"I . . . I think you're a strange person," she said, which should have been safe enough. Most people don't mind being called strange; in fact they would rather be considered a little strange and interesting than perfectly dull and normal. I told myself the girl meant nothing by the remark.

I said dryly, "Whether I'm strange or not, you're safer with me this minute than you would be just about anywhere else in the world, considering the fact that if I wasn't along you'd undoubtedly be sticking your neck out in some public-spirited damn fool way. I'm just about the only person in the world with whom you are safe right now."

"You don't really expect me to believe that?"

"No," I said. "But it would be better for you if you did."

"And easier for you!"

"Sure," I said. "But just keep clearly in mind one fact, kid. The one thing you know for sure about this deal—and I'm talking about knowledge and not guesswork—is that I could have let that jerk back there shoot you, but I didn't. That's the one cold, hard fact you've got. Don't let it get lost among a bunch of fancy theories."

She drove for a while, and glanced at me. "I . . . I don't understand," she said, a little uncertainly. "I mean, you *did* save my life, didn't you? I . . . it happened so fast I didn't really grasp. . . . But he *was* going to shoot me, wasn't he? Because I'd walked in there. And you shot him, instead."

"That's right."

"But . . . but the first shot; the one that made me open the door. . . . "

I said, "You'd be better off if you just forgot about that."

She said, "How can I? It happened, didn't it? You don't just forget. . . . The two of you were up in that room with a gun to kill somebody! Somebody out in the street!" Her voice was a little breathless.

I said, "You don't know that. That's theory, not fact."

"But I *do* know it!" she cried. "I heard the shot, didn't I? And when I opened the door, the other man was saying. . . ." She licked her lips and did not look at me. "He said triumphantly: *You hit him! You hit him! He's down!* I heard that. It's a fact. Isn't it?"

"Uhuh," I said. "More or less."

"Not more or less. Just fact. I heard it." She turned her head. "Who was it? Who did you shoot?"

I said, "You ought to do something about that curiosity. It's apt to be the death of you yet."

She shook her head abruptly, almost sadly. "You don't

make sense. First you save my life and then you threaten to kill me."

"I wasn't threatening," I said. "Turn in at the gas station up ahead; we're running dry. And this *is* a threat: if you try to signal the boy for help, he's apt to wind up dead. Even if you don't care about yourself, think about him and his wife and family. If he's got one. Take it easy and watch your step and don't try any gags about having to go to the john, in the hopes of leaving lipstick messages on the mirror. You might as well be learning to hold it for reasonable periods of time; you're a big girl now."

The movies and TV have done us desperate characters a big favor. They've built up the handgun in the public mind as a kind of magic wand; all you have to do to get the most amazing co-operation out of people is to wave a pistol at them. It never seems to occur to anybody that the only really effective thing you can do with a gun is to shoot it, and that there are times when this may not be desirable, profitable, or even feasible. The kid knew that I had the P-38 under my belt; but she also had some evidence to indicate that I didn't particularly want her full of bullet holes; and she might even have been able to guess that I wasn't anxious to damage any eager filling station attendants. Yet I had a gun, and by the code of TV that gave me the right to give orders; she would have been letting Hopalong Cassidy down if she had challenged my authority. She drove up to the pumps and sat demurely beside me with her hands in her lap while the man filled the tank. It was twilight now; and the sky ahead was painted with dramatic colors shading from crimson through orange and yellow to blue and purple. Strains of music reached us from a radio inside the station. Then the announcer began to speak.

"We interrupt this program," he said, "to bring you the latest development in the attempted murder of Governor Martin Maney. The getaway car in which one of the would-be assassins made his escape has been found abandoned by the State Police near the small town of Chaney Junction, forty miles south of Capital City. The police of neighboring states have been alerted to watch for the fleeing criminal, described as small and swarthy, wearing a light suit and a panama straw hat with a light band." I noted with interest that they were using Tony's description, not mine. "The authorities are confident that he will shortly be brought into custody—"

There was some more, while the attendant asked if he should check the oil. I told him to go ahead, and picked up the smooth voice again: ". . . meanwhile Governor Maney, who recently announced his candidacy for the United States Senate, is resting more easily in a private room at Memorial Hospital. Doctors describe his condition as only fair, complicated by shock and loss of blood. There is some doubt whether it will be possible to save the Governor's right arm, which was badly shattered by the dum-dum bullet used by the hidden marksman.

"The murder attempt took place at three o'clock this afternoon as the Governor, following his usual custom, walked from the State House to the Executive Mansion on Prince Street, accompanied by an aide. Alert police guards immediately located the source of the shot as a window on the third floor of the Wadsworth Building, and stormed the place before a second shot could be fired. One man was caught making his escape and was killed in a brief but savage gun battle. He has been identified as Samuel Banks, a small-time hoodlum with a long criminal record. The police are making an investigation of Banks's known associates, in an effort to place responsibility for the attack on the Governor's life. We return you now to our program of music for the dinner hour."

I put my hand on the girl's arm as she started to speak impulsively. She checked herself, sitting quite rigid beside me. I gave the man a five dollar bill for the gas and oil. We waited for the change; I didn't want him to remember us, even with gratitude. The colors were fading from the sky ahead as we drove away. I had her turn into the first small side road we came to. We were starting down a hill toward a wooden bridge, doing about thirty-five, when she jumped.

I made one desperate stab and got her wrist as she was going out. The car was gaining speed down the hill now. There was not much room for wrestling, but she did her best. I hung on grimly. The hand brake was, of, course, over to the left, far out of reach from where I was sitting; that's a little design feature a Detroit engineer is going to have to explain to me some day. I got my other hand on the wheel and pulled. Fortunately there was no ditch; just a ten-foot dirt cutbank. The right front fender took the shock.

Then we sat there for a while. I had hit the dashboard

with my shoulder; she had caught the steering wheel in the ribs. Her hat was coming off, her jacket was up around her armpits, and her skirt was up around her hips. I looked at her, feeling sad and misunderstood, like a boy with a pet robin that keeps beating against the cage. I released her wrist. She rubbed it mechanically.

"Why ... why don't you kill me?" she whispe   'Why don't you just kill me and get it over with?"

I said, "Why don't you just relax, kid?"

"You've got to kill me," she breathed. "Do you think I don't know that you've got to kill me? I'm a witness. I saw you in that room with the gun right after the shot. I heard what the other man said. As long as I'm alive, you can't even wriggle out of it by blaming him."

"Who's wriggling?" I asked. "Who's blaming? I shot Maney. I don't deny it."

She drew a long, ragged breath. "I know who you are!" she cried. "You're one of Gunderman's men! *Now* go ahead and kill me!"

Modern methods of news dissemination are wonderful. Here was this kid who, by her own admission, hadn't been in Capital City long enough to find out where to go to the bathroom, and yet she knew all about crime and politics. She knew all about Carl Gunderman, although she had never seen him and would not have recognized him if she had passed him on the street. She knew that anything that went wrong anywhere in the state, in a criminal or political way, was probably due to Gunderman. Any dubious character, in Capital City or elsewhere, particularly if he packed a gun, was apt to be on Gunderman's payroll. If the Governor was shot at, Gunderman undoubtedly had a hand in it. Well, as a matter of fact, he did.

I looked at her for a moment longer. It was obvious that we had reached the end of the line. If she was going to throw herself out of moving cars to get away from me, I might as well turn her loose and let her take her own chances.

I said, "Give me your purse."

She found it, and passed it to me. I located the driver's license. She was Barbara Elizabeth Wallace, white, female, five-five, a hundred and ten pounds, born the twelfth of March 1939. I had been a year or two off on the age. The address given was an RFD number near Grantsville, a small town in the southern part of the state. Apparently she had not lived in Capital City even long enough to have it changed on her license, as the law required. I tossed the stuff into her lap.

"Who lives in Grantsville, kid?"

She hesitated. "My sister and her husband and the children."

I glanced at the rings on her hand. "Where's your husband?" I asked.

"In Viet Nam," she said stiffly, and added after a brief hesitation, "He . . . won't be back."

That, too, made a difference, although there was no reason why it should. I asked, "Has your sister got more sense than you have?"

She did not answer, and I went on: "I'm giving you up as a bad job, kid. You might as well get your head shot off as break your neck jumping out of cars. But I'll give you a little advice. Go to your sister's and stay there. Write Mr. North Star Insurance that an emergency has come up at home and you're sorry but you've got to quit on him. . . . Where have you been staying in town?"

"At the Y on Seventh Street."

"Okay. After a couple of days you can write them the same story. Ask them to send your stuff home. Then sit tight and keep your mouth shut. It'll be a strain, but you never know what you can do until you try. I'm leaving you the rifle. Hide it somewhere. The reason I'm leaving it with you is that I can't very well carry it on the bus; besides, with your overdeveloped conscience you'll undoubtedly want to make a big gesture if an innocent person should be arrested. The gun's your evidence; you can march into a police station with it any time and create a sensation." I stripped off my gloves and dropped them into her lap. "Here's some more evidence, full of nitrate and stuff that the police chemists can have fun with. My name is Nyquist." I spelled it for her. "Paul Nyquist. I have a little gunsmithing business out on Western Boulevard. It is, of course, only a blind for all kinds of wicked and illegal operations. A bright girl like you can figure that out. A bright girl can figure out a lot of things that don't happen to be so. Keep that in mind before you rush out to get me thrown in jail."

I opened the door beside me. The bank made it a tight squeeze, but I managed, and walked around the car. The fender was crumpled, but I thought the wheel was undamaged.

I came back to her window. It was getting dark now, and her face was only a pale oval in the opening.

"You . . . you're letting me go?"

"That's the idea," I said. "I just want you to remember a few things. First, nobody knows you're involved except Whitey, you, and me. Whitey's dead and I'm not apt to talk. That leaves it up to you. Second, if you talk, you won't accomplish a damn thing. This deal is cut and dried, believe me. That is, it will be settled without any evidence from bright little girls with long inquisitive noses. In fact, such evidence will be very embarrassing to some important people—people who don't like being embarrassed. In fact, if you talk you will almost certainly be killed, and not by me. I won't have a thing to do with it. If you back up a bit, I think you can get out of there all right. Sorry about the fender."

I watched her out of sight. Then I turned and started walking.

chapter four

THE BUS got me into Poplar Island at ten o'clock at night. The bus station, in the center of town, was also a filling station and hamburger joint. I didn't need gas, but I was hungry. However, it seemed inadvisable to call attention to my arrival by going inside the place; besides my digestion might be better after I had learned something about the local situation. Or worse. I stretched to loosen the kinked muscles of my back and rear, tucked my shirt into my slacks, fastened my jacket over the butt of the P-38, and walked out the road on the left hand side facing traffic, as a battered sign advised. That being Saturday night, there was quite a bit of it to face. I tried to ignore the headlights lunging past from both directions; you'd think that a man who has been telling himself for a couple of years that he has nothing to live for would be able to keep his reflexes in order. But the instinct of self-preservation is strong in the human animal; and a couple of times it took everything I had to keep me from hitting the dirt at the sound of a truck exhaust.

Poplar Island is not an island but a peninsula; and while there may be a few tulip poplars still around, most of them have been wiped out by the promoters who have turned the old fishing village into a beach resort. I think there must be some kind of significance in the fact that no builders, contractors, or architects can stand the sight of a living tree. They don't even, it seems, dare go near the proposed building site until the bulldozers have scraped away the last vestige of anything green. Perhaps there's some kind of guilt complex at work here; they have been responsible for the consumption of so much dead lumber that they don't want to be reminded of the live thing from which it came. Or perhaps they simply don't want to have to admit to themselves that the place looked a lot prettier before they stuck up their damn little pastel-colored cracker-box shacks.

I saw the sign of the tourist court up ahead. I've heard there are one or two in the town that won't take couples in cars with in-state license plates unless they can display wedding rings showing a reasonable amount of wear, or other evidences of respectability. This joint wasn't one of those. In fact, I had been told that on week-ends during the season three or four cabins are never rented to overnight guests, despite the demand; they're reserved for short-term business from the neighboring beer hall. That, of course, is merely hearsay and I can't vouch for it personally. There are some people who can see sex in everything. It's surprising how often they are right.

My car, one of those little Plymouth station wagons, was parked in front of No. 14. There wasn't much light; I had to guess at the color and the dented rear fender and the printing on the door: *Nyquist and Hoffmeyer—Custom Gunsmiths.* But it was the right kind of car in the right place. I stood in the shadow of a tree—there were some left this far out of town—and looked at the lighted window of the cabin and wondered who was inside. There was only one practical way to find out. I checked the loads in the P-38, tucked the weapon back under my belt but did not button my jacket, and walked forward.

It was my car, all right. I moved past it to the cabin door. There was no point in being cute about this. The gun in my belt was just moral support; it wouldn't mean a damn thing if the verdict back in Capital City had been thumbs down. In that case there would already be a gun out in the dark somewhere, aimed at my back. I turned the knob. The door was unlocked. I walked in.

The man lying on the nearest bed said, "What the hell kept you?"

I had never seen him before, but there was something familiar about him: he was about my size and his hair was about the right color. Otherwise he had a kind of pansy look that was reflected in his clothes and I would have hated to think the resemblance was a close one. But you had to admit the organization was pretty good. Everything was thought of, except the possibility of failure; and I had no doubt they were working on that now. I would learn the answer soon enough; but apparently not tonight. Tonight, it seemed, we were just putting the train back on the tracks and getting it on schedule again.

I said, "I'm here, aren't I?"

He said, "Well, it's nothing to me as long as I get paid, except that I missed my plane."

"They'll have another reservation for you," I said.

He got up and put on a jacket and went to the door. "It's all yours," he said. "But you ought to get those front wheels balanced. The heap shakes like a paint mixer at seventy."

I said, "There's no law saying you have to drive seventy."

We looked at each other for a moment longer. I knew I would never see him again. He had been hired for the job from a long ways off: man wanted, five-eleven, a hundred and seventy, regular features, blond, unknown locally, fee and expenses paid. Now he was going back where he came from. Or perhaps they would take him out in the Bay and drop him overboard. I didn't know. From the faint uneasiness in his eyes I understood that he wasn't quite sure, either. There was always a possibility, on a job like this, as he knew much better than I. After all, I had only been actively engaged in the business for some seven hours, measured from the time I had first pulled the trigger of the Springfield this afternoon. Up to that moment I had been only a kind of honorary and associate member of the underworld. Now I was a criminal establishing an alibi. It didn't seem to make much difference. Nothing had made much difference to me, for a couple of years now.

The man in the doorway looked at me, and grimaced, and

said, "If I'd known I was supposed to look like a college boy, I'd have told them to go to hell."

I watched the door close behind him. Then I turned to the girl who was curled up in the chair in the corner, her legs dangling over the wooden arm. It didn't seem as if the position should be a comfortable one, in theory, but she looked comfortable enough. She was small, almost tiny, with short black hair cut in a bang across her forehead, and a little upturned nose, and a small, pouty mouth. She was wearing high-heeled white sandals, a strapless print dress with a full skirt, and blue nylon panties with pleated ruffles. Her position facilitated a complete inventory, leaving only the question of a brassiere for later determination. After I'd had my look, she giggled and tossed her skirt over her knees.

"Hi," she said. "I'm Jeanie."

"Good for you," I said. "I'm Paul."

"He was cute," she said. "Did you have to send him away?"

"Three's a crowd," I said.

"I like crowds."

The repartee was getting excruciating. I asked, "Have you had anything to eat?"

"Who wants to eat?" She picked up an empty glass from the floor beside her and held it out. "Be an angel, angel."

I took the glass and set it on the dresser beside the half-empty fifth and the pitcher of melting ice. "I want to eat," I said.

"I don't think I'm going to like you." When she pouted, her mouth only got more that way. You could hardly tell the difference.

"It has happened before," I said.

"What?"

"Never mind."

They had opened my suitcase to get the liquor out. I went to it and found a sports shirt. This was no community for a coat and a tie; besides, I had been sweating all day with a coat on. I tossed the P-38 into the suitcase and dropped the lid on it. The girl got to her feet and disappeared into the bathroom. The weapon may have had something to do with her sudden decision. She came out shortly, working her lips together to distribute the fresh lipstick, paused in front of the dresser mirror for inspection, went back to her chair, and picked up a length of printed material identical with that of her dress, but fringed at the ends. She draped this about her shoulders, and returned to the mirror to check the result before pronouncing herself ready.

I took her to the hotel, where I knew the food to be edible. Afterward we progressed into the bar. Despite her head start, it took me until two-thirty a.m. to get her drunk. She passed out in the car on the way back to the tourist court. I parked in front, carried her inside, kicked the door shut, and dumped her on the farther bed. She was out cold. I started to cover her up the way she was, but a glance around told me that she had brought nothing down here with her besides one tiny overnight bag; apparently the dress she was wearing was going to have to do another day. I therefore removed her shoes and rolled her over. She unzipped down the back; the rest was no more trouble than skinning a rabbit.

I pulled a sheet over her, and hung the dress in the closet, trying not to remember another girl for whom, for a brief period of time, I had once done similar favors, but under more legitimate conditions. I got into pajamas, went to bed, and concentrated on not thinking about anything, particularly the fact that I was not alone in the place. It was certainly a hell of a way to be crippled; and having a bunch of surgeons tell me that the first guy had done a beautiful job after it happened, and there was nothing organically wrong, didn't make it any better. Those medical characters all stick together, anyway. I'd had six months of practical proof they didn't know what they were talking about.

chapter five

WHEN I WOKE UP, at six-thirty, she was still asleep. I shaved, showered, got into old clothes, and drove into town. The only place open for breakfast was the bus station hamburger joint. It wasn't as bad as it looked. I had them make up some lunch and fill the Thermos while I was eating. Then I drove back to the cabin. The girl rolled over and looked at me when I came in. She sat up, pushing her fingers through her hair.

"Wha' time zit?" she asked, yawning.

"Quarter of eight," I said. "I'm going fishing. Get some clothes on if you want to come along."

"Quarrer a eigh'!" she said. "Fishing! Oh my God!" The last words came out nice and clear. She turned away from me, laid herself down, and pulled the sheet over her. Well, there was nothing in the instructions that said I had to carry her around in my pocket. In fact, there had been nothing in the original instructions about her, period. This was supposed to have been a fishing trip and nothing else. She was just a cute wrinkle somebody had thought up later—and I could guess who.

I got back in the car and drove down to the water and rented a boat with an outboard motor. Two kids, about twelve and fourteen, were fishing off the pier. They already had the bleached, towheaded look that kids get in the summer, although it was barely July. They watched me load my gear into the boat with silent interest.

"Come along," I said. "Show me where." I could not quite face spending the day with no one but myself and some fish for company.

The kids looked at each other.

I said, "My name's Nyquist. I'm staying out at the Rainbow Court." I took a dime out of my pocket and tossed it. The older boy caught it. I said, "Find a phone and check with your folks. Tell them we'll be in by three; I've got to get back to the city this evening."

They ran off together, pausing by the station wagon to note that at least one of the names on the door checked with the name I had given. Smart kids. I lit my pipe and got my tackle ready. Personally, I don't consider fishing much of a sport. For one thing, most fishing tackle is flimsy, spindly, characterless, mass production stuff. For another, a fish is, in my opinion, a poor excuse for something to eat. However, I like to get out on the water occasionally. Today wasn't just one of the days, but it was better than staying in the cabin with Jeanie and her hangover.

The two boys came running back. It was okay, they said. They got their tackle into the boat. One of them promoted a dollar from me and disappeared, returning with a carton of Cokes and some change. I pulled the starter cord and we were off. It was a fine day with only a light southerly breeze, so we headed out into the Bay. I was sleepy and had a bit of a hangover myself; I let the boys handle the boat and the time passed in a kind of peaceful haze. I did not make much of a reputation for myself as a fisherman. The older boy brought us back in only a few minutes after three. There was nobody in the cabin when I returned to the Rainbow Court.

The beds were made. The girl's dress was gone from the hanger in the closet. Her little overnight case, open, stood on the straight chair by the window. A towel and a bathing suit, both wet, had been dropped in the middle of the bathroom floor. I picked them up. The suit was white, sandy, and diminutive. I frowned at it thoughtfully. She was not a girl I would have expected to go in for solitary swimming. Well, her presence here wasn't my idea. People who dreamed up gags like that could damn well worry about their backfiring; I wasn't going to, at least until I'd had a shower.

Despite the fact that I had spent quite a bit of time outdoors that spring, a day on the water had left me moderately sunburned about the face and arms. I know that doctors have proved the destructive effects of ultra-violet upon the human epidermis; nevertheless, a little sunburn always makes me feel healthy. I dressed in slacks and my gaudiest sports shirt—fairly conservative by local standards—and got into the car. There wasn't a great deal of choice; Poplar Island isn't Atlantic City by a long shot. Smitty's Pier seemed like a good place to start looking.

It's on the river side of the peninsula, just off the highway; in fact you have to park on the left and walk across. The Pier is a long shed of a building built out over the water, surrounded by a board walk from which people fish in the daytime and on which they neck at night. I make the latter statement from observation, not from experience. The place was crowded—mostly, it seemed, with children: sunburned, sticky, sandy, clutching Coke bottles, Good Humors, and ice cream cones, along with fishing rods, sand toys, and inflated plastic and rubber devices in all shapes and sizes. The parents had withdrawn into the corners to drink beer. Down at the end of the long, dark, noisy room, a juke box was going. She was there, all right, dancing with a thin young man with red hair and freckles, wearing gold-rimmed glasses. He had a country look, like a farm boy in town for Saturday night; you expected him to go in for sleeve garters and chewing tobacco. You had to hand it to the girl. She could really pick them.

I could not help grinning at the thought. I leaned against one of the six-by-sixes that held up the roof and watched them. It was a style of dancing that I had never mastered, having been an inhibited youth. They were working hard and sweating at it; and every time the girl spun so that her dress flew up, the sailors in the nearby booth would cheer. She spun fairly often. Then the juke box ran down and while somebody was feeding it nickels the two of them dropped down at a table occupied by some paper plates, glasses, half a dozen empty beer bottles, several full ones, and the girl's purse and stole—if that's the proper word for the length of cloth she picked up and draped around herself before sitting down. I walked across to join them. The juke box started up again but nobody paid it any attention. The girl looked up quickly as I sat down.

"Hi, stranger." Her eyes were faintly uneasy. She had been a naughty girl and she knew it. "How was the fishing?"

"Lousy," I said. "Not that it makes any difference. I can't eat the damn things anyway. They make me sick." I turned to him. "Hi, Jack."

"You boys know each other?" the girl asked, even more worried.

"Sure," I said. "I've known Jack a long time. How's the big crusade, Jack?"

"Still crusading."

I spoke to the girl. "Jack's paper's got a mission. They've been bucking Martin Maney since way back before my time here, when he was State's Attorney. They consider him a kind of potential Hitler, I gather; they've been exposing his high-handed, dictatorial, arrogant police-state methods for years. The adjectives are the *Courier's*, not mine. What burns them up is that Maney seems to be smart enough to stay honest so they can't pin anything on him except that he's been a little rough on a few crooks and racketeers in his attempt to clean up the state. For further details, I refer you to a daily column called *The Grapevine* by Jack Williams—"

I saw her reach for the glass, but did not bother to try to stop her. It's not much of a trick to accurately heave the beer out of a glass in a given direction; it's a lot harder if you try to throw glass and all, which is what she did.

The glass went past Jack Williams's ear. The beer distributed itself impartially over all of us including Jeanie herself.

"A reporter!" she gasped. "A lousy damn reporter! I'll—"

We were all standing up now; and people were looking at us. I got behind her as she went for him, hauled her back, and rammed her down in the chair. "Sit down and mop yourself off, honey," I said. "You smell like a brewery."

Jack was wiping up the table with paper napkins. He sat down again, took off his glasses, and polished them with a handkerchief. The girl subsided and started to dry her hand and arm with Kleenex from her purse. I had got some on my shirt, but I didn't figure a little beer was going to affect the pattern adversely. It was that kind of a pattern. Jack put his glasses back on. The incident did not seem to have disturbed him. I guess he was used to having girls throw beer in his face. He leaned forward and said seriously:

"The analogy with Hitler is very sound, as a matter of fact. Sound enough, at least, that we can't risk letting a man like Maney get as far as the United States Senate. In some respects I suppose it's unfortunate that the lad who took a crack at him yesterday was a lousy shot."

These idealists are all alike. They talk big about democracy but they're always willing to have a political figure they don't like removed by any nice convenient undemocratic means, like a rifle bullet.

I said, "Well, what brings you down here, Jack? Business, or—" I glanced at the girl, who had conjured up another full glass from somewhere and was staring into it, pouting. "—or pleasure?"

He said, "Well, as a matter of fact, I wanted to talk to you about this Maney business."

I grinned at him. "Honest, officer, I've got an alibi." I was enjoying myself. When you've got nothing to lose, you can take your kicks where you find them.

He laughed. "Yes. I must compliment you on your taste in alibis."

I said, "Honey, the man's flattering you."

"I'd like to flatter him," she said. "With a broken bottle I'd like to flatter him! A lousy damn reporter!" She emptied the glass and looked around for something with which to refill it. I pushed a beer her way.

Jack said, "Well, as a matter of fact, I talked to the editor about doing a column on it, Paul, and your name came up. I called your place and your partner said you'd gone down here for the week-end. When I got here this morning, you were out fishing, so—" He shrugged. "Well, the young lady said something about a swim, and it seemed like a fine idea. One thing led to another. I hope there are no hard feelings."

"None on my part," I said. "I can't speak for Jeanie. Her pride is hurt. She thought you loved her for herself alone. Right, honey?"

"Oh, shut up."

Jack said, "As I say, Paul, I talked it over with the editor. We found ourselves stumbling over some technical questions, and there didn't seem to be anybody around who knew any more about firearms than what button you push to make a service rifle go boom. You seemed to be the logical person to give us a hand. You know as much about guns as anybody around; or a little more. How about it?"

I said, "On or off the record?"

"Off, if you prefer."

"I prefer. I wouldn't want to be quoted as contradicting some police ballistician. There's a lot of room for argument in this stuff, you know."

"Check. I'll leave your name out of it. Now, first of all, what do you think of the guy's shooting?"

I grinned. "According to the radio, Maney's still alive. The shooting was terrible."

"A man's a mighty small target at that range," Jack said.

He was just as cute as a little red wagon. I said, "Well, let's just figure the range. From the Wadsworth Building down Lincoln Avenue to the corner of First Street, right? That's what the man said on the radio. That shouldn't be much over three hundred and fifty yards; four hundred at the most. Hell, in the Marines we did regular target practice up to six hundred; sometimes we shot at a thousand, just for fun."

Jack said, "Actually, the range was a little over four hundred yards. I paced it myself yesterday."

I said, enlightened, "Oh, then Maney must have been standing on the north side of the street. I was just figuring to the corner." This was more fun than fishing. I said, "Well, let's look at it another way. Just an average good bolt action hunting rifle with store-bought ammunition will usually keep its shots within two minutes of angle, or about two inches at a hundred yards, measuring from center to center of the bullet holes. That's eight inches at four hundred. Of course, the dispersion will be somewhat greater at the longer range; on the other hand, if this guy knew anything about guns at all—and particularly if he loaded his own ammo—he could cut that figure down considerably. Just a little work bedding the barrel and action properly into the stock would improve the accuracy a lot; a little more experimenting to find out the particular load the musket liked best would cut the dispersion by several inches at four hundred yards—"

He looked up from the notes he was making. "You mean there's a difference between bullets?"

I said, "Between bullets, cases, primers, and powder. Mostly you work on the powder. Which powder and how much is the big question, although the choice of bullets is also pretty important."

"And anybody who wants to do accurate shooting has to load his own cartridges?"

"That's right," I said. "Either that or get some friend with a loading press to do it for him. Except for .22 shooting, there isn't a top ranking target shot in the country who uses commercial ammunition, as far as I know. The commercial stuff's reliable, of course, but in the nature of things Remington and Winchester can't tailor it to your particular gun; and every gun is different."

"Then you'd say that the man who shot Governor Maney probably had access to a—what did you call it—a loading press?"

I said, "Maybe. But you've got to remember that he missed. We don't know what kind of a shot he was. He just got the arm, he must have been ten or twelve inches off the mark. Anyway, there are quite a few people loading their own these days, just as a hobby. I guess there must be several dozen just among the guys who drop into the shop. A large percentage of our custom-built rifles are for cartridges the manufacturers never heard of. We make up the brass and load it for the customer on order; but usually he winds up buying an outfit and loading for himself. It's a simple process, once you have the tools. Hell, the old buffalo hunters only carried a handful of cartridge cases. Every evening they'd sit down and reload the ones that had been fired during the day." I grinned. "Besides being simple, it cuts the cost in half, or better. You pay for the tools in no time, if you do any shooting at all."

Jack scribbled notes. I poured myself some beer. The girl beside me did likewise. Jack looked up. "What about the chances of matching the bullet to the rifle?" he asked. "I understand that's quite a science these days."

I shook my head. "You're thinking of revolvers and pistols. Most handguns give a muzzle velocity of less than a thousand feet per second. The chances of finding enough bullet to match up with the barrel aren't as good as the detective stories would make you think; but there's a reasonable possibility. Most rifles, however, push their slugs along at well over two thousand feet per second. Some go as high as four thousand. When a rifle bullet hits—particularly if it meets up with a bone—it's usually mashed up enough that you can hardly tell what caliber it was originally, let alone what particular gun it came from. If Maney's arm was mangled enough that there's some question of his keeping it—as I heard over the radio—then I think the chances of the police doing much of anything with the bullet are very slight."

"So that the killer could safely keep the gun in his possession?"

"Unless he left some brass around. *That* could be matched to the bolt head and firing pin of the gun."

"Brass?"

"Cartridge cases."

"Well, if there were any cases found in the room, the police are keeping it a secret," Jack said. "Now, what about the bullet. Some sections of the press and radio are making a big thing out of its being a dum-dum bullet. They claim that only a fiend who really hated Maney's guts—"

"They're nuts," I said. "Most bullets are dum-dum bullets. That's just a fancy name for an expanding bullet; which is precisely what you buy when you walk into the store and ask for a box of thirty-thirties. You don't want a full metal-jacketed bullet that'll punch a neat round hole through your deer and let the poor beast run away somewhere to die a lingering death; in fact, full-jacketed bullets are illegal for hunting in most states. What you want is a soft nosed slug that'll spread out and kill on the spot, and that's what you get. The only bullets that aren't dum-dum, if you want to call it that, are the ones specifically designed for target shooting—and military bullets, which by international agreement can't be of the expanding type. But you'd have to look hard to find full-jacketed ammunition for the average gun. The guy probably used an ordinary hunting bullet. It doesn't mean a damn thing."

Jack made some more notes. "Well, let's see what we've got here. You'd say that a good shot should be able to keep his bullets within an eight-inch circle at four hundred yards—"

I shook my head. "That isn't what I said. I said that's what the *rifle* should be able to do. On top of that you have the question of what the man can do. It would depend on his eyes, what kind of sights he had on the gun, whether he was shooting from a rest—"

"A table with a small sandbag was found in the room."

"Well, if he was shooting from a rest, with telescope sights, and the gun was properly sighted in, then he might figure on eight inches at four hundred, *if* he knew how to shoot and had plenty of sleep the night before and didn't get buck fever at the last moment, which is not out of the question. After all, it's one thing to shoot at a piece of paper or a tin can or even a deer, and another to shoot at a man. My own impression. . . ." I hesitated.

"Go on."

"My own impression, just from what I heard and what you've said—that sandbag sounds professional enough—is that we're dealing with a reasonably good shot who could probably have drilled Maney dead center if he'd been a paper target. But since it was Maney, the pressure was too great and the guy lost his nerve at the last minute and flinched the shot off. At that range it only takes a twitch of an eyelash. After all, if he wasn't rattled, why didn't he fire again and make sure. He'd know that he had missed—"

"How? Maney was knocked down by the bullet. The man might have thought—"

I said, "Don't be silly, Jack. Anybody who's done any shooting knows where his shots are going. Even when you pull one way out, you still know just about where it's going. Unless, of course, the sights are off. But I think the guy just flinched on his first round and then said to hell with it: he didn't really want to shoot any governors that day." Anyway, it made a good story.

chapter six

HALFWAY BACK to the city she had to stop at a filling station. It seemed that I was doomed to associate with people who couldn't wait till they got home. I pulled up tactfully at the pumps, although the tank was three-quarters full. The man managed to squeeze four gallons into the Plymouth; he couldn't find room for any oil or water. It was not a bad little car. I paid for the gas. The girl came running back, banged the door shut, and curled up on the seat beside me. She had been out in the sun enough today to turn pink; she looked hot and damp and rumpled and a little subdued. I found her more attractive that way; I found myself idly visualizing the possibilities of a couple more bottles of beer and a blanket on the beach.... Well, it was no use dreaming. I had made enough of a fool of myself along those lines, a couple of years back, to last a lifetime. I put the car in gear and took us away from there. We didn't talk much on the way to town.

She lived, I had already been told, in an apartment with two other girls in one of those old blocks of brick row houses on the west side. I understand they used to be desirable residential properties at one time. I pulled up to the curb, walked around to open the car door for her, and carried her little overnight case into the vestibule.

"Well," she said, "well, thanks a lot, Paul. I had a swell time."

"It goes double," I said.

"See you again real soon," she said. "Give me a ring."

"I'll do that."

She was looking up at me, I saw, a little too closely; and I knew what was in her mind. She wanted to know, just for the record, just what the hell had happened between us last night after she drew a blank. I put an arm around her and kissed her and put the suitcase into her hands.

"So long, Jeanie. Take care of yourself."

Driving away, I wiped my mouth off and looked at the

lipstick on the handkerchief and grimaced. It seemed appropriate that the stuff should taste of raspberry.

The shop is just a couple of blocks from Lincoln Avenue on Western, in the short business section out there, before Western widens out to become a boulevard with a park down the middle. The location is good enough for us. Downtown might look better, but people with guns to be repaired like to park close so they don't have to walk too far with everybody, policemen included, looking and wondering what bank they're planning to rob. For a country once referred to as "a nation of riflemen" we're certainly making it tougher every day for anybody who wants to learn to shoot, or having learned, to keep his hand in; which seems a little stupid, considering the state of world affairs. . . . Well, don't let me get started on that. I parked in front. There was a light in the shop. I went inside. Hoffy was busy checkering a Mannlicher-style stock in walnut: a nice, straight-grained piece of wood. A boy of about fifteen was sitting on my workbench, watching.

"Customer for you," Hoffy said, looking up briefly to jerk his head toward the kid.

I said, "Hi, Dick. What's the trouble?"

The boy said, "Well, I think I must be jinxed or something, Mr. Nyquist. I tried to shoot my qualification again this afternoon. I had seven shots right in there and then the damn firing pin broke on me. I tried to finish up with Bobby Stein's gun, but. . . ." He shrugged wryly.

"Tough," I said. "Where's the gun?"

"Right here." He slid off the bench and turned to pull the rifle out of its case: one of those Mossberg .22-caliber target models that are a hell of a lot of gun for thirty dollars. I was glad to see that he opened the bolt before handing the gun to me, as he had been taught. I did not ask him what was so desperate about a broken firing pin at this hour of a Sunday evening, when he wouldn't get out to shoot again until next Sunday. I'd been a kid with a gun once myself. After all, who was going to protect his home against burglars if his gun was out of commission? And if the Russians dropped the bomb on Capital City during the week, who was going to feed the family on pigeons and squirrels from the park and fight off looters and fifth columnists and paratroopers until order was restored? I mean, it was an emergency. "Do you think you can fix it, Mr. Nyquist?"

"Sure," I said.

One good thing about mass-production is that the stuff comes through simple. Most of the latest designs are really very neatly put together; you can get into them with no trouble at all and hardly any tools; a change from some of the old timers that are real bastards to work on. I had this bolt apart and back together in short order. The kid watched me closely; next time he would know how to do it. I shoved the bolt into the gun and gave it back to him. He hesitated, and I knew he was waiting for the bad news. I looked it up in the parts list.

"A dollar forty," I said.

"I . . . I'll have to pay you next Sunday, Mr. Nyquist."

"Sure."

I watched him case the gun and run out, after thanking me. I made a little note in the book: *Dick Mancuso—$1.40.* They all paid, when they remembered; and I made sure they did remember, for their sakes as well as for my own. Hoffy made some growling comment behind me.

I said, "Shut up, Hoffy. Those are the boys who are going to be buying your fancy Mannlicher stocks twenty years from now."

"Meanwhile you fix their guns for the price of the parts."

"It's an investment," I said. "We'll get it back."

I stood for a while watching him work. To me, checkering on a gunstock is like the pink ribbon on a Christmas package—pretty, but I'm more interested in what's inside. I've never had a gun slip in my hands because it wasn't checkered; and at one time I had the opportunity, along with a few million other men, to fire a good many rounds through the unadorned weapons provided by Uncle Sam. I'm strictly a barrel-and-action man myself. The only things that interest me about a stock are the way it fits the metal parts and the way it fits me. However, there are people who consider fine checkering an art; and among these people Gustaf Hoffmeyer is considered a top-flight artist. He also has a special, secret oil finish that has made the antique-loving wives of some of our customers weep bitter tears that it should be wasted on a nasty old piece of wood fastened to a nasty old gun; and he can do a job of bluing that'll knock your eye out.

Hoffy was from my home town, never mind where. Because

of his manner and appearance—he looks like a fat Prussian pig with a grouch against the world—he wasn't doing very well; people liked his guns but not enough to put up with his rudeness and temperament: in particular, the fact that he was unreliable as hell about deliveries. I talked him into coming to Capital City with me. We made a pretty good team and the business was coming along to the point where we had recently hired another man, a young fellow named Hines, to take the job of routine repairs off our shoulders while we concentrated on the custom-built rifle angle. Of course, during the hunting season, we all repaired guns. That was the one big drawback to the business; you had a hard time getting out hunting yourself for keeping other hunters' guns in working order.

Hoffy said. "Two calls while you were gone. Some reporter with foolish questions. Did he find you?"

"He found me."

"Also a girl."

I knew an odd little feeling of anticipation, and worry.

"What girl?"

"How many girls you got, hey? This is the Plaza 3-3039 girl, and you better wipe the corner of your mouth before you call her back. Some women got eyes that can see along a telephone wire. Her I did not tell where you were."

"Good enough," I said flatly. I did not ask myself what other girl I had thought might be calling. "Thanks, Hoffy."

"Better you get some sleep tonight. This job will be ready for sighting-in tomorrow and I don't want you scratching up my stock with your screwdrivers."

I laughed and said, "Steady as a rock, Hoffy. Steady as a rock. Don't stay up all night, yourself. Remember it's Sunday."

He made a noise denoting the extent of his respect for the Sabbath. I went out the front door, got my suitcase from the car, and entered the door at the side of the building, which opened on a stairway, which led up to my apartment above the shop. It was a convenient arrangement. I left my suitcase by the door and went into the kitchen for a beer. Returning, I sat down at the desk in the living room and reached for the telephone. Marge answered the phone herself.

"Hi," I said.

"Paul, darling!" She always sounded very, very refined over the phone.

"What's the trouble?"

"He wants to see you."

"Where?"

"At the club. Come by and we can ride over together. Have you had dinner?"

"No."

"Don't. Make him feed.you. And, Paul—"

"Yes?"

"Don't worry. Everything's fine."

"I wasn't worried," I said.

She had a low, rich laugh. "Nothing worries you, does it?"

"What have I got to worry about?"

"Well," she said, "it's a point, but I wouldn't push it too hard, darling. Don't be long."

"Half an hour," I said, and hung up, and went into the bathroom, pulling off my shirt. My image in the mirror halted me. I reached for a towel and scrubbed the remains of Jeanie's lipstick from my mouth. The number of women with whom I was getting involved, in one way or another, seemed a little funny, considering the circumstances.

chapter seven

I TOOK a taxi over because there's never any place to park near the place. The doorman recognized me and spoke to me by name; the elevator operator said I looked like I had been out in the sun, Mr. Nyquist, and I agreed that I had. We agreed that it had been a fine week-end, the first in a long time. Any time the sun shines between Friday and Monday it's always the first fine week-end in a long time, unless it happens twice in a row, in which case it's a dry spell and the farmers need rain. I got off at the eleventh floor and walked down the carpeted hall. The door was unlocked. I went in. She called from the bedroom.

"Paul? Come on in, baby. I'll be ready in a minute."

Something about the prosperous apartment always made me want to move around on tiptoe. There was, however, no need for it. The rugs were so deep you couldn't make

a noise in hobnailed boots. I think it was the silence that
got me. Even the discreet whisper of the air conditioning
was a kind of silence, covering up the little outside sounds
that might otherwise have sneaked in. I glided soundlessly
through the open bedroom door.

She was sitting at the curved vanity table—a tall, willowy,
well-proportioned girl. When I had first known her she had
been a blonde; now her hair was dark, cut short, and curled
all over her head in the Italian movie-actress style, although
she was about as Italian as a pair of bluejeans. She was
also working on the sultry, sexy look to go with the hairdo.
For this she was a natural, blonde or brunette. She was
wearing, above the waist, a wired brassiere and a pair of
dangling earrings the clamps of which she was adjusting.
Below the waist she wore a starched white petticoat, nylons,
and high-heeled evening sandals. Somehow her incomplete
costume put me in mind of the scaffolding on a building
under construction. She turned and grinned at me.

"You're just in time to help me with this damn zipper,"
she said, rising. She looked ridiculous walking across the
room to the bed in the stiff petticoat: it was not a glamorous
garment. The nice thing was that she knew how she looked
and didn't care if I laughed. It was one of her good qualities.
There are very few good-looking girls who can stand to be
laughed at.

She picked up the pale green dress that had been laid
across the bed, pulled it over her head, and worked it
cautiously into place, sucking in her guts to give herself slack.
The dress was of some shiny material like taffeta; there
was nothing to the bodice, and a great deal to the skirt
although it ended a foot above the floor. The zipper was
under her left arm. I seemed to have got into a rut. If I
wasn't waiting for them to go to the bathroom, I was zip-
ping them up, or down. When I was finished, she lowered
her arm and let herself breathe again.

"You bastard," she said. "What are you trying to do, commit
suicide?"

"If I ever do," I said, "I won't ask anybody else to help
me."

"He was fit to be tied," she said. "What the hell happened,
anyway?"

"Things went wrong," I said.

"You can say that twice! Jesus Christ, man! I thought you could shoot!"

"I can shoot," I said.

"Why the hell couldn't you have drilled the little pipsqueak through the heart while you were at it? Instead of just shooting an arm off him? Now we've got real trouble!"

"Is he going to lose the arm?" I asked.

"Don't you read the papers?"

"No," I said.

"You screwball," she said. "You don't give a damn about anything, do you? No, they've got it sewed back on for him, but it's going to be a long time before he'll have full use of it again, and you know how that's going to make the little louse feel! Him and his tennis and his setting-up exercises. He's going to want blood, brother—your blood, if he ever finds out who was behind that gun. And he's taking it as a declaration of war, election or no election. The cops are clamping down all over the state—"

"Maney'll simmer down," I said. "He'd rather be Senator, in the long run. Now he's got it made. Hell, he can electioneer with his arm in a sling. A martyr to the cause of good government. I did him a favor."

"Uhuh," she said, "and he'll appreciate you with an axe, if he ever learns your name. In fact, you're pretty damn unpopular all over the place right now."

I said, "Sorry. I'll leave."

She grinned. We looked at each other for a moment. The high heels she was wearing put her face on a level with my own. It was a good face except for the mouth: gray-blue eyes with plenty of room between them, strong cheekbones, straight nose, firm chin. Even the shape of her head, revealed by the short haircut, was good. A lot of women look deformed when shorn of their hair. And under other circumstances I suppose I'd have had no complaints about the mouth, either. The weakness it betrayed—the slight, moist fullness to the lower lip that any man would recognize—was not, I was aware, considered a handicap in the circles in which she moved. It was all in the point of view.

"You bastard," she murmured. "I went to bat for you, you big lug. Carl wanted to throw you to the dogs, but I wouldn't let him." She put her arms about my neck and kissed me lightly, and ran her tongue across her lips. "I wish—" she said, and released me, and turned sharply away.

The elaborate full skirt of her dress whispered when she moved. I reached out and swung her back.

"Cut it out, Marge," I said. Every so often she had to dramatize the situation.

"Darling," she whispered, "when I thought you were dead . . . !"

"When was that?"

"Why, that was the first thing we heard! That Maney had been wounded but was still alive and that a man had been found dead in the room. Naturally everybody figured that Whitey had shot you and beat it. Baby," she said, "baby, I was *sick,* I really was! I hadn't realized how much I—"

I said, "Marge, don't make a production of it."

She was, I suppose, sincere enough in a way. She had probably felt—or thought she felt—all the things she said. She could usually kid herself into feeling just about anything she wanted to feel—and grief was a nice, noble emotion to play with. Now that I was back, alive, she wanted me to get into the act with her. When I laughed, she slapped me across the face.

She was no hothouse flower, and her swing had power behind it. I had met up with it once or twice before. It rocked me. She had not lost any strength, grieving for me. I caught her wrists; she fought me silently for a moment, straining against my grip, almost motionless but her long earrings swung and danced and caught the light. She ceased her resistance abruptly, letting my strength throw her at me. I had to release her wrists, and step back and brace myself, to keep both of us from landing on the floor. I saw that the anger had turned to a kind of malicious mischief in her eyes. She threw her arms about my neck and kissed me, deliberately moving hard against me. Sometimes there were indications that little Margie had a few medical theories about me, herself; I think she saw me as a kind of challenge—and there was no denying that if a cure could have been effected by that method, she was the girl with the equipment to do it.

I'd had a rough week-end, in certain respects. First there had been the girl in the blue suit. Then there had been the little chick they had wished off on me down at Poplar Island. Now here was Marge, playing games. I shoved her away from me so hard that, stumbling back against the bed, she fell full-length across it.

She did not move, lying there across the bed with her dress bunched about her and her legs dangling. She began to speak, softly, breathlessly, calling me names. I think she had a theory that if she could get me mad enough, interesting results would follow. It was no worse than a number of other theories I'd heard from more medically qualified sources, and no better. I walked into the living room while she was still talking, made two drinks at the bar in the corner, and went back into the bedroom. She had not yet run out of breath.

"Do you want to drink this, or should I just throw it at you?" I asked, standing over her.

She sat up hastily, and, after a moment, grinned. Then she took the glass, and drank, and looked up at me again. "I wish—"

"For God's sake, Marge. Play another record."

"Why did it have to happen to you? Why not to some crumb. . . . Ah, hell," she said, taking a deep swallow. "It's a lousy world, and look at that damn stocking. Well, maybe it won't run any farther." She got up and wriggled and pulled herself back into place inside the dress, which had slipped a little. "I look like the middle of winter," she said. "But if he likes it. . . ."

She shrugged. There was no need to finish. We were both aware that there were people whose idea of elegance did not include simple, summery dresses; besides, some men liked their girls shiny, both to look at and to touch.

"You should have worn a dinner jacket," she said. "He likes people to be dressed up in the club."

I said, "When I met him, he hadn't shaved in a week. I'm clean and respectable. I've got coat and tie on. Finish your face and let's go."

chapter eight

HER CAR was a long, pale-blue Cadillac coupé. She always drove it just as hard as the automatic transmission would let her, which, in a Cadillac, is hard enough. The doorman jumped to help us out when we slid to a stop in front of the Oasis Club. Inside, the air conditioning met us coldly, which must have been a relief for her, what with the silver foxes she had draped about her. We went on through to the rear. There were a couple of jerks in the outer office. There were always a couple of jerks in the outer office. We started to go in. One of the jerks looked up.

"Wait a minute," he said, and came over, and started to frisk me.

It was a sign of something or other; it hadn't happened since the first time I had come around, two years before. I raised my arms obligingly, and drove my heel down on his instep. It was a new pair of shoes, and I hadn't got around to having rubber heels put on them. The jerk screamed. The door opened. Brooks came out, and pulled the door shut behind him.

"What the hell's going on here?" he asked. The jerk was hopping about on one foot.

I said, "I'm sorry. I must have stepped on his toe by mistake."

The door opened again, and stayed open. Carl Gunderman was leaning against it in an idle sort of way, creating some doubt as to whether the door could take it. He looked a little as if he might absently pull it off the hinges and start folding it like a match cover, just for something to do. He was a big man.

"What the hell goes on out here?" he demanded. "What the hell's Corky doing, playing hopscotch? Goddamn it, I try to run a quiet, refined place here and then my own boys start raising hell like it was a south side saloon."

Marge said, "He started to frisk Paul—"

Gunderman said, "Brooks, get the stupid bastard out of here before I get mad and break his other foot." Brooks, a tall, thin, blond man of about forty, hesitated noticeably; he had never liked me and he wanted to protest. He liked to consider himself Carl's right-hand man, and maybe he was. Certainly I had no designs on the job. Finally he jerked his head at the man called Corky, and they went out together. Gunderman looked at me, and grinned, "Feeling tough, eh, boy?"

He knew why I had done it: to prove to myself—and perhaps to him—that I was still man enough not to have to take anything from any of the back-alley creeps that hung around this place. It amused him, and I didn't mind. I knew something about him, too.

"Not tough," I said. "Just ticklish."

He laughed, and turned to the remaining jerk. "Tell Raoul to put the steaks on. Three. We'll eat out there. . . . Honey, you look swell," he said to Marge, putting his big hand on her waist and drawing her hard against him as he turned. "Come on in and have a drink, Paul."

I followed them through the door. Walking ahead of me, they made a touching picture of affection, if you want to call it that. I half expected to hear her purring like a cat. I knew too much about their relationship; they both seemed to get a kick out of confiding in me. Watching them together in the evening was always, to me, like watching the preliminaries between a pair of large wild animals. In the morning, if I wanted to, I would be shown the bruises and the teeth marks and the wrecked clothing. They knew all about me; and I knew all about them: so much that my life was never quite safe. It was all that kept things interesting, nowadays. It was a game I had played for two years. Some men climbed mountains for excitement. Some men hunted big game. Some fought bulls. I was a friend of Carl Gunderman's. Well, I suppose you could call it friendship, although there were times when I woke up at night and played with the thought of killing him, and I was reasonably sure he felt the same about me.

But it was too late for killing; much too late. There had been a moment, two and a half years ago, when I could and should have shot him—not necessarily through the heart, just through the leg or shoulder, to bring him down. I woke up, sometimes, thinking of that, too. But it was too late now. For me. It was different with him, and I had no doubt he had some night thoughts on the subject, from time to time. Some day he would come to a decision. Meanwhile we were pals.

I watched him go over to the portable bar now, to mix the drinks; all two hundred and sixty-five pounds of him, only a little of it fat. He was quite a sight in a white dinner jacket; he had been even more of a feast for the eyes when I had first met him, wearing some outfitter's idea of a hunting costume, at a lodge down in North Carolina. That much man draped in red-and-black wool plaid is something to see. You'd never mistake him for a deer, which I guess is the idea.

You never know who you're going to meet at a place like that. There may be a serious trophy-hunter or two, after bigger heads to mount and hang on the gun-room wall. There'll be a few nuts like myself, trying out the latest wrinkle in rifles and cartridges. There'll be the get-away-from-it-all boys who simply want to commune with nature for a couple of weeks each year—I don't know why this always involves leaving the razor at home. And then, of course, there are always the bottle-babies, to whom a hunting-trip without liquor is unthinkable; they'd sooner leave their guns behind than the case of you-know-what.

It should come as no surprise to anyone when I say that Carl Gunderman and the two jerks he had brought with him for protection and company fell into the last category. When I arrived, they were making a big uproar about the liquor laws of North Carolina—as if the proprietor of the lodge were responsible for this peculiar legislation. For the next two days they were more concerned with the problem of replenishing their dwindling supply than with the problems of hunting. After that, they began to gripe about the lack of game to shoot at, which was something that disturbed us all. The guides were doing their best, with dogs and without, but anything they started invariably took off in the general direction of Tennessee, and we never got a glimpse of it.

Ordinarily I don't think much of organized hunting. For any game with which I'm reasonably well acquainted, I prefer to dive into a country alone—or with one congenial companion—and play it by ear. To sit on a windy ridge in late fall, with a trigger-happy stranger somewhere on my left and another somewhere on my right, waiting for somebody to chase something shootable my way, isn't precisely my idea of Heaven.

This was a special situation, however, and a species of game I had never encountered before—which was why I had saved my pennies and ditched a week of law school to make the trip. We were not primarily after deer, although the season was open and nobody intended to pass up a buck if one showed himself. We were after a quaint beast known as the Russian wild boar, not to be confused with the razorback hog which, in various degrees of wildness, is to be found all through the south. The Russian boar, an import from Europe, flourishes only in this one small mountainous corner of North America. It is not a domestic pig gone wild, but a real boar, with hair, tusks, and temperament dating back to prehistoric times.

It is probably the only game animal on the continent which, given a choice, will charge a human being. This, Carl Gunderman told me privately, was why he had come here. There wasn't much sport, he said, in mowing down an inoffensive deer with a high-powered rifle; a peaceful black bear wasn't much better, even if you could find one; and grizzlies were practically non-existent except in Alaska—and who wanted to go clear to Alaska for a bear-skin rug? He, Carl Gunderman, didn't like shooting at anything that couldn't fight back; which was why he had considered that hunting was strictly for squares until somebody had told him about these ill-tempered Russian pigs. . . .

I listened to this routine, with variations, for several days. Personally, I don't consider hunting a contest between man and animal; to me, it's a test of skill, just like golf or bowling. If I do a clean job, I win; if I mess it up, I lose, even if luck helps me to wind up with a trophy regardless. To me, hunting is marksmanship spiced with tracking and woodcraft; it's a game, and there's nothing like it. I realize that a good many people consider this a cruel and heartless attitude, since the life of an animal is involved. They have a point, and when they stop eating meat slaughtered for them in the stockyards, I may stop shooting my own. Meanwhile, I just want to make it clear that I don't go hunting to risk my life. There are too many ways of dying without looking for more, as I discovered during my stint in the service. But if Carl Gunderman, fortified with whisky and with a .30-30 in his mitts, felt that he was proving his courage against that of a pig, I had no intention of arguing with him.

As you will gather, I'd had the luck to draw him as a partner. The choice had not been mine and certainly not his; things had just worked out that way. I have always been a strong walker; and Gunderman, despite his drinking, was the only other member of the party who could keep up with the guides. The weaker sisters—including the two jerks and an old gentleman with a bad heart—thus found themselves stationed along the lower parts of whatever ridge, valley, or mountain we happened to be hunting that day, while Gunderman and I invariably wound up on top, through a process of natural selection. He wasn't going to let himself be out-walked by a couple of hillbillies—as he referred to the guides—or, he implied, by any damn college student, either; while I had hunted enough to know that we were much more likely to find game higher up.

We had therefore struck up a friendship of sorts, based on necessity and mutual tolerance. He was really quite an interesting man to talk to in a way; I learned things from him on the subject of the law, for instance, that would have startled the professors back at the University. He also could, and did, discourse extensively on the subject of women. We got in the habit of leaving our stands to eat lunch together; occasionally we'd look each other up during the long, cold afternoons, to exchange sarcastic views about the hunting and the weather, and have a nip out of his flask to ward off the chill. To me, he was a fascinating specimen; to him, I guess, I was a stuck-up intellectual punk; however, I did know more about hunting and guns than he did, so that made us even.

The week drew on without anyone seeing a sign of deer, bear, boar, or any other game, legal or otherwise. On Thursday, the dogs picked up a trail and followed it out of the country; the guides came in well after dark, exhausted, grabbed something to eat, and drove off to borrow another pack somewhere. I never did learn whether they ever retrieved the first bunch. They were good men and they were working themselves mercilessly, but the game, if any, just wasn't co-operating. Friday we were up before dawn—except for a couple of fellows who said to hell with it, they were going down below the lodge and shoot grouse. The rest of us headed into the mountains again; and Gunderman and I again wound up together, this time on a thinly wooded saddle well above snow line. It was hard finding anything dry to sit on.

We had our lunch and griped about the prospects—guides and dogs had long since vanished into the wilderness to the west—and went back to our stands. I had been careful, in choosing my own location, to place a rocky knob between myself and the big guy. If he did see something to shoot at, I didn't want any thirty-thirty slugs rambling through the sparse woods in my direction. Until I've seen a man behave in the face of game, I never trust him very far with any kind of firearm: some people can get awful damn excited. It was close to three o'clock, and almost time for us to start heading back down if we were to reach the cars before dark, when I heard the dogs in the distance.

Let me say here that I'm a bird-dog man myself. Hounds, in general, mean nothing to me; and this business of turning a bunch of mutts loose to chase something up a tree—coon, possum, bear, cat, lion, or what have you—is my idea of nothing to do. I'm stepping on a lot of toes when I say it, but I go hunting to shoot, not to chase through the woods after a bunch of yelping canines.

Nevertheless, I must admit that after a week of waiting, there was an undeniable thrill in hearing the pack heading our way in full cry; and I went through the motions of checking the rifle and scope—I was using a privately souped-up version of the .300 Magnum, with a two-and-a-half-power glass—and made sure that I was standing where I had a clear field of fire along the ridge, and particularly into the little dip that looked to me like the kind of easy spot an animal on the run would pick for crossing from one valley to the next.

At first, however, it seemed as if the chase was bearing to my left, and Gunderman would get the shot. The dogs were really sounding off now; the one that seemed to be leading the pack had a ringing voice that came close to making me forget my anti-hound prejudices. He was really carrying a tune. Abruptly, they all switched direction in the scrub below me; then the whole mad orchestra came charging toward my private little notch; and now I could hear the crashing and thumping of whatever was in front of them. I had shot my first buck when I was twelve, and I had hunted ever since—even the war could hardly be considered a lay-off—but I had to admit to myself that I was sweating a little as I waited for the shot.

A breaking stick behind me brought me around sharply, and the gun came up without conscious effort. I suppose the dogs's racket had got on my nerves; I guess I had a vision of a boar slipping around in back of me while I watched the trail. Gunderman's gaudy costume may have saved his life; I had the crosshairs in line before I recognized the red-and-black plaid in the scope.

"What the hell are you standing there for?" he yelled at me. "Come on, let's cut them off!"

He had no business leaving his stand, of course; that was the way people got themselves shot. I lowered the gun, and

watched him rush past me and down the slope. The impulse
to finish the move I had started, and put a bullet into his
broad back, wasn't strong but it was there. After all, this
was *my* stand.... I saw the boar come into sight below.
I spat the bad taste out my mouth, and lifted the rifle again;
with the scope-sighted Magnum, good for five hundred yards,
I could pick the animal off before Gunderman could bring
his short carbine into play. The idea was tempting, but the
big guy was floundering around down there, and I wasn't
quite angry enough to shoot that close to another man; not
here in the woods where a bullet could ricochet off a limb
in any direction.

I lowered the gun, therefore, and watched him set himself
to shoot. He was about fifty yards away. The boar was plainly
in sight now, weaving through the scrubby trees below. Still
worried by the pack behind, it had not yet spotted the man
in front. It was an ugly beast, black and hairy; two hundred
pounds of prehistoric pig, with upcurving sickleshaped tusks.
Lumbering along uphill, it made a beautiful shot; the range,
for Gunderman, was less than a hundred yards already. I
waited for the report of the thirty-thirty, but no sound came.
Then I heard a metallic clicking noise, repeated, and looked
at the big guy.

He was standing there, with boar coming on, sighting very
carefully; then he levered the shell out of the chamber without
pressing the trigger, and drew a bead again; and again he
flicked out the loaded shell, never realizing that he had not
yet fired a shot. Like I say, they get excited. He must have
pumped half a dozen loaded cartridges through the mechanism
before the truth dawned on him.

It hit him suddenly. He looked down at the unfired gun.
Then he stared for an instant at the approaching boar. Then
he threw the gun aside and ran.

The movement—and perhaps the bright plaid hunting
clothes—caught the pig's attention at last; the beast broke
stride. You could almost see the little eyes narrow with delight.
The head came down, and the boar charged. I placed the
crosshairs on his shoulder, not trusting the soft-point bullet
to penetrate the skull. As I held my breath, steadying,
Gunderman blundered directly into the line of fire, and almost
took a bullet for a second time in as many minutes.

The rest was the kind of nightmare you hope to forget.
I remember shouting at him to get the hell out of the way;

if he had run any direction but straight at me, it would
have been easy. But he was deaf with panic and came
blundering on; and behind him came the boar, only faster.
I remember my first incredulous realization that somebody
was going to get hurt here unless the damn fool got his
hulking big frame out of my sights. It seemed idiotic to
have to stand there with thirty-five hundred foot pounds of
energy in my hands—enough to shoot through three pigs
lengthwise if it didn't hit too much bone—and not be able
to use it; yet every time I sidestepped to get a clear shot,
the big lummox veered toward me. When he reached me,
so help me, he grabbed for me instead of going on about
his business.

I struck him with the gunbarrel, although it was no way
to treat a fine weapon. I have no idea how hard I hit him
or where he went to after that. Fighting free of him, I
slipped in the snow and fell; and looked up to see the boar
almost on top of me. I rolled over, found the gun I had
dropped, and managed to fire once before the tusk went
into me. I remember thinking it was a hell of a silly way
to die—but of course, I didn't die. I was still alive, in a
manner of speaking.

chapter nine

NOW I LOOKED at the big guy, standing in his gold-plated office in his gold-plated nightclub—he had another place on the
edge of town, but the Oasis was his pet because nice people
came there. The secret was ours; his and mine. He had
told some story about a jammed gun. Whatever the guides
had made of the sign in the snow, they had kept their mouths
shut; and Carolina was a long ways off. His secret was
safe, except for me.

I had, of course, been in no condition for a press conference
when they got me off that mountain; they had barely managed
to keep me alive with transfusions, I learned afterward. I
had not talked later. It wasn't the sort of story you wanted
to broadcast about another man without good reason. For
me to shame Carl Gunderman publicly just to pay him back

for what had happened to me would have been childish. It wasn't as if he had caused it deliberately.

We had never even referred to it between ourselves; it hadn't happened, it didn't exist. He had come to the hospital when I was convalescing, and we had chatted about this and that—mostly football, it being still that season of the year—and when he had decided I wasn't going to bring it up, he said, "Look, boy, what're you going to do now? Go back to school?"

When I said I could see no reason why I shouldn't, he said, "Well, if you change your mind, I've got a proposition for you. There's a gunsmith who's been wanting to retire, in my town, and you like that kind of work, the way you used to talk out there in the woods. If you change your mind, just say the word and I'll buy the place. You can pay off as you make it; slow or fast, any way at all. Meanwhile, don't worry about your bills here; they're all taken care of. I'll be seeing you."

He walked out before I could protest; it was his way of acknowledging a debt, I suppose, and offering payment. He always prided himself upon being a guy who paid off in full. I did not think the offer to set me up in business was wholly disinterested; doubtless he had some notion of keeping me and my knowledge under his eye. At the time, the idea of becoming a gunsmith had seemed mildly fantastic. I had more ambitious plans. That was in the fall. It was early summer, I remember, when I called him long-distance to ask if the offer was still open.

I watched him now, big and smooth and handsome in his white dinner jacket, mixing the drinks with one arm around the girl in the shining pale-green dress with whom I'd recently been doing some wrestling myself. I thought he would laugh uproariously when he heard about that—and she was just the girl to tell him. He had a great sense of humor, as long as the joke was not on him. We had come a long way from that snowy ridge in North Carolina.

I want to say this: I never hated him—except sometimes at night. I always tried to remind myself that what had happened to him that day could have happened to anybody; it could have happened to me, except that I'd been hunting since I was a boy and had got the buck fever out of my system. It takes more than just nerve to do the right thing at such a moment; it takes experience and practice. It was highly possible that Carl could go out tomorrow and shoot five charging boars stone dead without turning a hair—although I did not really believe it, and neither did he, which was another reason he wanted to keep me around. Some day, somehow, he was going to prove to both of us that it had all been a big mistake.

There were times when I could not help feeling sorry for the guy. To be that big, to have shot your mouth off that much, and then to have to remember yourself running like a scared kid. . . . I sometimes thought that was why he behaved the way he did with Marge. There is a certain mentality that equates courage with sexual prowess; perhaps he was reassuring himself that since he had plenty in the one department he could not really be lacking in the other. Well, he probably had some fancy theories about me, too; although he was not what you'd call a theoretical character. Practical jokes were more in his line.

I said, "Carl, what was the idea of sicking that little girl on me?"

Marge looked around. "Who, me?"

I said, "No, not you, honey. I said a little girl."

Gunderman was grinning. "How'd you make out?" he asked, reaching out to put a glass into my hand.

"Swell," I said. "Just swell. Couldn't have done better." Which was the literal truth.

Marge asked, "What the hell is all this?"

Gunderman laughed. "Oh, I just thought that Paul ought to have a better alibi than a bunch of fish. So, I fixed him up."

My affliction, you must understand, was something we kidded about freely among the three of us, although it was a secret from the rest of the world. Carl had passed the word to Marge when she became curious about me; at the time, I had resented this, but now I was glad that she knew. It made two people in the world with whom I could act wholly natural.

"You fixed me up, all right," I said.

He was still laughing. "What did you do, boy, make like a gentleman?"

"Don't be silly," I said. "She wouldn't have known what I was talking about. Fortunately she wasn't bashful about accepting drinks from strange men. I poured her into bed about three o'clock in the morning." I tasted the contents of my glass. "You sonofabitch," I said mildly.

"Don't be sore. What's a little joke between friends."

I said, "As long as we *are* friends. Are we, Carl? The goon at the door didn't seem to know about it."

Marge said, "Ah, don't talk stupid—"

Gunderman said, "Shut up, you." She shut up. He looked at me for a moment. "Well, what do you think?"

I said, "It was a question I was asking myself about three-oh-five yesterday afternoon."

"And the answer, boy?"

"The answer was, I didn't know. I wasn't quite sure how much your friendship was going to stand, Carl. So I laid low until I heard over the radio that you hadn't thrown me to the wolves after all. Tony was still taking the rap, in absentia. It seemed safe, then, to carry on with the assignment as originally planned."

Gunderman said, "You made a lot of trouble for me. Not leaving the gun. Not taking the car. I had to scramble, I tell you, to clean up after you. Where's the gun now?"

"In a safe place," I said.

"All right," he said, "don't tell me. Play cagey if you like. But it might help if we could feed it to the cops at the right time, to keep them on the right trail. And off the wrong one. If you know what I mean."

I said, "If we need the gun, I can produce it."

"Where were you between three and ten o'clock, Paul?"

"Around," I said. "Around and around."

He said, "How'm I going to trust you, boy, if you don't trust me?" He was cute when he got that plaintive note in his voice, all six feet six of him. I grinned. He laughed shortly. "Okay. Okay. Now, what happened?"

"What happened?" I said. "The shot was a little off, that's what happened."

"It wasn't supposed to be off, boy. I gave you a high recommendation. I said you could part a man's hair at half a mile and never crease the scalp. How do you think this makes me look?" He wheeled on me abruptly. "It makes me look like a damn double-crosser, that's how!"

"I'm sorry," I said.

"I hope you're sorry!" he said harshly. "I hope to God you're sorry. But it would be nice if I could be sure." I did not speak, and he said, "If I thought you'd crossed me deliberately—"

Marge said, "Carl, you're—"

He turned on her. "I told you to keep your trap shut! Get out of here and see what's holding up that damn cook; he's had time to grow those steaks from a calf." She hesitated, made a face to show her independence, and went out. He waited until the door had closed. "All right, Paul," he said. "Spill it."

I said, "The little sap didn't stand still. I figured he'd at least have sense enough to hold his pose for the first one. I was going to put it right by his ear, to make it look good. He wanted them close, didn't he? I was going to put it a foot from his ear; and then put another a couple of feet high as he hit the cement; and then splash a few around the sidewalk for effect. So the dope started waving his arms like a windmill just as I fired. The slug was clear by a good twelve inches, but he reached up and picked it out of the air. That's my alibi, Carl. You can take it or leave it."

After a moment, he grinned. "Ah, hell, boy, don't get your back up. You can see how it is, can't you? A lot of plans were hanging on that shot; Maney's and mine both. When he came to me with this publicity stunt idea, I thought he was cracked. But the papers had been riding him; the *Courier* in particular. They were claiming that his anti-crime crusade was a fizzle; they were even hinting that he was a loudmouthed hypocrite, playing ball with the underworld. Imagine that; suspecting our Governor of associating with racketeers! Some guys have real imagination, eh, boy?" He laughed. "Anyway, the little twerp wanted something fancy to throw the press off the trail; and we cooked this up between us. If the criminal element hated him enough to want to kill him, he couldn't be in league with them, could he? I told him he was safe like in church; that I had a man who could make Deadeye Dick look like a snotnosed kid with a BB gun. I didn't tell him your name; we agreed that if he didn't know, he could do a better job of acting when they started hauling in suspects. Besides, I didn't trust him—although I didn't say that." Carl made an abrupt gesture. "But now you can see how it looks. Now he thinks I had a bright idea and decided I was going to run the damn state by myself. He thinks I gave you orders to shoot to kill; and he's out to pay me back if it wrecks the machine and the party and his own career."

I said, "He'll get over it. When it comes to deciding between ambition and revenge, it isn't even a choice, for Martin Maney."

"Yeah," said Carl, "but while he's making the choice, he's costing me money."

I said again, "I'm sorry," and I was. It had started out as an interesting project—professionally speaking—and a favor to Carl. The political and moral aspects hadn't concerned me; what did a man in my shoes have to do with politics or morals? That was for people with a stake in the future that I could never have. But now the thing had got out of hand, and grown, like a snowball, to landslide proportions; and I realized that I should have known better than to get involved in a gag like that. Whenever you start horsing around with guns something always goes wrong.

Carl clapped me on the shoulder. "Ah, hell, boy, forget it." We were pals again. He fixed me a new drink. "What happened with Whitey?" he asked.

I said, "Whitey got excited when Maney keeled over, and pulled out a gun. It didn't seem to occur to him that I was sitting there with a loaded rifle in my hands. I turned it around and squeezed the trigger. I never liked the jerk, anyway." I glanced at him to see if he realized that I was leaving something out, but he just grinned at my callous recital. I said, "What about Whitey? Is anybody likely to want to take it up?"

"Around here?" Carl laughed. "Whitey was strictly expendable. Don't give it a thought."

"What about the police?"

"They've claimed him, haven't they? Didn't you hear it on the radio? That lets you out. They can't very well arrest a guy for killing a guy they claim to've knocked off themselves in a savage gun battle." He chuckled. "You know cops, particularly Capital City cops. Always eager to get some credit. And they needed some credit with Maney getting shot under their noses. Besides, one of the boys who got there first was on the payroll. He did some quick thinking; it was his idea to empty a couple of police .38's into the stiff and call it a gun battle. The two cops with him thought it was a swell idea; and the department bought the story and gave it to the papers. Now they're stuck with it. No trouble there." He gave me a sideways look. "What's with Jack Williams?"

"The usual," I said. "Questions."

"What brought him snooping around Poplar Island?"

"Jack talked it over with his editor," I said. "A column. About the shooting. With a technical slant. They needed advice. They thought of me. Would I mind giving them a little information? Off the record, if I preferred. About guns. Nothing but guns."

Gunderman grimaced. "I suppose he talked to that little tramp about guns, too."

"For that information you'll have to see her," I said. "She was your idea, not mine."

"Didn't you ask?"

"And build it up to something important?"

"Okay," he said. "I'll look into it. And Williams, too. That boy has a bad habit of sniffing around the right holes. One day he's going to crawl down and find something. It'll be tough if he never comes up again."

I said, "If anything happens to Williams, I'm through."

There was a silence. Then Carl said mildly, "Don't get tough with me, boy."

I looked at him for a moment, and he knew what I was thinking, and his face changed. It was kind of an ugly moment. I said, "I'm not tough, Carl. I'm tender as one of your five-dollar steaks. But leave Jack Williams alone. It's bad business getting rough with reporters, and I want no part of it."

Then Marge came in to say that dinner was ready. Afterward I left them. The doorman wanted to call me a cab, but I told him I needed fresh air. I'm still a pretty good walker. The Oasis Club is in the middle of downtown. The city seemed quite dead, so late on a Sunday night. I took First Street across to Lincoln, without thinking much about where I was going, except that I was moving in a general homeward direction. It startled me to find myself standing on the stretch of sidewalk that I had been watching through a six-power telescopic sight some thirty-odd hours ago. The yellow fire hydrant was an old friend; I had focused on it several times. I looked down at the pavement beside it; the dark stains of Maney's blood were clearly visible, seeming melodramatic and improbable. I couldn't work up any sympathy for the little man; after all, he had asked for it.

I crossed the street and walked out Lincoln on the right hand side. The window was still open about a foot; perhaps its position was being preserved as a clue. Across the two windows to the left I read: *North Star Insurance—J. R. Fenwick, Agent.* I hoped to God the kid would have sense enough to keep her mouth shut, but I wasn't betting on it.

Hoffy was gone when I looked into the shop. The Mannlicher stock was finished, a sweet job. I sat down and assembled the gun, just to see how it would look all put together. Hoffy can visualize them, but I have to see them. It was a lovely thing, a gun we could be proud of. I hung it on the rack and went upstairs. Grace's picture, affectionately signed, watched me from the bureau as I undressed. She had been a lovely thing, too, and doubtless still was, somewhere. I kept the picture around to remind me not to make that mistake again, doctors or no doctors. I turned out the light and went to bed.

chapter ten

WHEN THE doorbell awoke me, I had that feeling of having momentarily lost touch with time. I did not know whether a minute had passed since I fell asleep, or an hour, or the whole night. Then I realized that it was still dark outside. I looked at my watch. It read a little after one. I had been in bed only a couple of hours. The doorbell rang again.

I yawned, turned on the light, got out of bed and put my feet into a pair of moccasins. The only trouble with the place is that you have to go down the stairs to open the front door, and then you're practically standing in the street. I looked around for my light dressing gown, and remembered that it was in the suitcase, which I had not yet unpacked from Poplar Island. When I hauled the robe out it uncovered Whitey's P-38. The bell was still ringing impatiently. The pistol seemed, for some reason, like a good idea. I tucked it inside the waistband of my pajamas, belted the dressing gown over it, and went out through the living room and down the steep stairs and pulled the door open. Marge was standing there. The light from the street was behind her, of course, so I could not see her clearly, but she seemed to be dressed pretty much as the last time I had seen her. She took a step forward; and suddenly she was in my arms.

"Paul!" she gasped. "Oh, Paul!"

I patted her shoulder through the furs, and reached down to pull the gun out from between us as it started to slide down inside my pajamas. Now it seemed like a silly thing to have brought along. I closed and latched the door.

"Come on upstairs," I said, and followed her up. There was light in the bedroom but none in the living room. I laid the gun aside and reached for the switch.

"Oh, don't!" she whispered. "Don't turn on the light, baby. I look so—"

I said, "Relax, Marge," and pushed the switch.

She turned slowly to face me, a little defiantly. After a moment she let the foxes slide off her shoulders and trickle to the floor, so that I could get the full picture. Aside from the furs, she was wearing only the green dress, her evening sandals, and one earring. I don't know what made it so obvious; I think it was the lack of stockings that made the biggest difference, that and the limp straight way the dress hung about her without support from underneath. The dress itself was badly crushed, and a drink had been spilled on it, and it was ripped, on the left side, from the top of the bodice almost to the knee. He could just as easily have reached a little farther and pulled the zipper, but it had probably been more fun this way. Four small safety pins held the torn cloth together after a fashion. Her sandals had been buckled but the ends of the straps were not tucked in. Her mouth had a bruised and swollen look.

I grinned at her. "Did you get the number of the truck?" I asked.

"He . . . he raped me!" she whispered. "Damn it, he *raped* me!"

I could not help laughing. "Marge, for God's sake. This is Paul, honey. Remember me?"

When she moved, it was somehow even more apparent that she was wearing nothing under the ruined evening gown. She was a little unsteady on her feet. She swung away jerkily and walked to the end of the room.

"Get me a drink."

"Sure."

When I put it into her hand, she said, "What's between you two? What did you say to him, anyway? There wasn't anything to get ugly about, was there?"

"Did he turn ugly after I left?"

She nodded. After a moment she said, "What's Jack Williams to you, anyway?"

"Did Williams figure in it?"

She nodded again. "He didn't like your standing up for him. That started it. It just went on from there, kind of. The big ape! I'd like to. . . . Ah, hell!"

"What happened?"

"Look at me," she said. "Do you have to ask?"

"Marge," I said, "who're you trying to kid, anyway? Remember New Year's Eve? It was a week before you could see out of that eye—"

"Yes," she said, "and he was sorry as hell about it, too. Do you understand? Even when it happened, drunk as he was, he knew he'd hurt me and. . . . Damn it, baby, it's not *what* he did tonight, it's the *way* he did it! Like I was just something to be tossed on a bed and stripped and ravished—"

"Ravished," I said, laughing. "There's a nice word, ravished. Marge, you're getting to be a poet."

"You bastard," she said, and then she grinned at me. "Okay, so maybe I'm taking it too big. But I didn't like it, see? I don't mind if he wants to play it rough. I like it rough, as long as I don't get marked up and he pays for the damages. But I want to be there, see? I want him to know it's me. Damn it, Paul, I love the guy. I . . . I'll be anything he wants; anything he needs; but you'd damn well better not tell him I said so. But as long as there's two of us in the room, he can do what he damn well pleases. But when he closes me out. . . ." Her mouth trembled. "Ah, hell," she said. "I must be drunk."

There was a little silence. I think we were both somewhat embarrassed. Love had never before figured prominently in our conversations.

Presently I asked, "Where's he now?"

"Still at my place, I suppose, unless he's waked up," Marge said. Her voice was casual and disinterested. It struck me, suddenly and hard, that she was lying. She went on: 'He was pretty drunk. He passed out, afterward. I managed to pick up my dress and shoes and sneak out without disturbing him. I found some pins out in the kitchen. My wrap was lying in the living room. The garage keeps the keys to the Caddy. It's a damn good thing because my purse had got kicked under the bed and I didn't have a cent for a taxi."

I looked down at her curiously. She had found a chair and was sitting there with a kind of defiant gracelessness, her crumpled taffeta skirts hanging down between her bared knees. She was making a production of it, I realized; and I did not believe in it. That is, I had no doubt Carl had given her a bad time; but I was fairly certain that, whether he was still at the apartment or not, she could have managed to lay her hands on some presentable clothes, had she wanted to. She had not wanted to. She had preferred to appear before me like this. It put a different light on the situation. Of course, I had to keep in mind that she did like to dramatize herself. It could be no more than that.

I put my hand on her head and closed my fingers, not hard, on the rumpled dark curls, and pushed her head away from me so that her face turned up. I looked down at her a moment longer, and grinned.

"Marge, you're cute," I said.

Her eyes wavered; then she laughed. "Don't you start mauling me, you big bastard."

I released her. "I suppose you want to stay here. Take the bedroom. I'm a gentleman. I'll sleep in the study."

She finished her drink and set her glass on the floor and got up, hesitated, and walked to the bedroom door. Then she turned back to face me, and I could see the familiar look of mischief—not altogether nice—that had come into her eyes. She lifted a hand deliberately, caught the bodice of her dress, and pulled. The safety pins ripped out and the abused evening gown opened up like a shell. She let it drop about her feet and bent down to unfasten her shoes, straightened up and stepped out of them, away from the clothing on the floor, and posed for me in the doorway, smiling as she removed the remaining earring. She tossed it to me. I caught it.

"Think what you're missing, baby," she said.

"I think of it," I said. "Occasionally." I took off my dressing gown and tossed it to her, in return. "In case you want to bring in the milk in the morning," I said. "Good night, Marge."

"Paul."

I looked back. She had thrown the light, striped seersucker robe over her shoulders and pulled it about her.

"Yes?" I said.

"I'm sorry, baby. I shouldn't tease you. That's dirty."

"Good night."

When the door had closed, I let the grin slide off my face. I looked at the earring in my hand, recognizing it. I had given her the pair for Christmas. Come to that, she had given me the dressing gown. Carl had given me the Plymouth I was driving these days. He went in for big presents. I'd had Hoffy restock a Winchester Model 12 trap gun for him, and worked over the action myself, not that Carl was much of a hand with a shotgun—any gun, for that matter, although he liked to think himself pretty hot with a pistol. But he showed up at the gun club occasionally, and it was the best I could manage.

They were all the family I had. They were the only people in the world with whom I could be natural, because they knew all about me. I did not have to put on an act for them. I did not have to wonder how much they guessed, or how they would behave toward me if they knew, because they knew.

I went into the study, threw a sheet over the studio couch, found myself a pillow, and slept until daylight. I was awakened by the sound of a police siren stopping in the street outside.

chapter eleven

THERE WAS no reason, I suppose, why it could not have been a fire engine, an ambulance, or even a kid with one of those gadgets on his bicycle. Nevertheless, I knew it was the police, and I swung my feet out of bed, and yawned, and scratched my head, and listened to the sound dying away outside. At least life wasn't dull these days. All you had to do for a little excitement was take a shot at a governor. Any old governor would do.

I couldn't seem to get very concerned about it. They were

ringing the doorbell now. Marge had my light dressing gown.
I found my heavy wool robe at the back of the study closet
with my winter suits, and pulled it on. The living room,
when I came into it, looked kind of stripteasy, to coin a
word. I picked up the furs she had dropped the previous
night, and her dress and shoes. The dress still had a stiff
shell-like look, like something shed by a large insect. The
long tear disclosed the inner engineering of the bodice: the
seams were reinforced with flexible white stays. I had always
wondered how they kept the damn things up. I opened the
bedroom door and pitche˙ ˙˙˙ clothes inside and pulled the
door closed.

They were still working at the doorbell. Somebody was
telling somebody to get around back, which seemed a little
silly. If I'd been going to leave, I would have done so when
I first heard the siren. I got the P-38 off the table and
hung it on the rack on the far wall where I keep my personal
guns. It had plenty of company there: four rifles, two shotguns,
and my .45 and .22 automatic target pistols. I wasn't very
concerned about it; if they knew enough to trace it back
through me to Whitey, they knew too much already. Besides, guys like Whitey very seldom carry traceable pistols,
and there was no sense in acting like this was a detective
story of some kind. It wasn't going to be solved by clues.
My life did not depend upon clues, but upon people and
what kind of deals they had been making. It would be
interesting to see how it worked out. It wasn't much of a
life, anyway. I went down the stairs and opened the
door.

"Not so damn fast," I said, when they started to barge
in. "What's the trouble? This is a hell of a time to be
waking people up."

The man in charge was a detective lieutenant named Fleet,
a good-sized man, middle-aged, sandy-haired, with very cold,
pale blue eyes. You noticed the eyes. You noticed the face,
too. They all, after they have been on the force for a while,
get a kind of deadpan look. It's almost like a disease of
the skin of the face and the underlying muscles, as if a
surface paralysis had set in so that, while they can still
smile and even laugh upon occasion it has to come up from
underneath and break through a kind of crust of impassivity.
I had met Fleet before, when we ran off some pistol matches
for various organizations around town. He was a good shot,
for a cop. Today he had another plainclothesman with him.

A third man was falling over garbage cans in the narrow alley between the buildings.

Fleet backed up. I removed the foot with which I had blocked the door, and let it swing open, but did not step aside.

Fleet said, "Which is your car, Mr. Nyquist?"

I said, "The blue Plymouth over there. Why?"

Fleet said over his shoulder to the man behind him: "Check it."

I said, "What's going on here, Lieutenant?"

"I'd like to talk to you."

"Here?" I asked.

"Downtown." When I hesitated, he said, "I haven't got a warrant and it's not an arrest."

"Okay," I said. "Come on up while I get dressed." Walking up the stairs ahead of him, I asked, "Are you going to tell me what the problem is, or am I supposed to guess?"

"You're supposed to guess," he said. "It's part of the technique. It puts pressure on the suspect. He talks too much, trying to find out what not to talk about."

I said, "Oh, so I'm a suspect."

"Uhuh," he said, still behind me. "Where were you last night, Mr. Nyquist?"

I tried not show surprise. I hadn't been thinking of last night. "What time last night?"

"Any time."

I turned to face him in the living room, and watched his eyes look the place over, not missing the guns, or the highball glass that Marge had left on the floor beside the chair at the end of the room.

I said, "I got a home a little after seven, changed my clothes, and took a taxi over to the Lordsley Apartments to visit a friend. We went to the Oasis Club for dinner. I walked home; got here somewhere between ten-thirty and eleven, I think. Here I am. Does that help?"

He shook his head. "Not much." He looked at the glass by the chair again. It was standing in a little pool of water caused by condensed moisture due to the ice that had been inside, now melted. I could not see if Marge had left any lipstick on it; she had not had much to leave, as I recalled. I wasn't greatly concerned about her reputation. Considering everything, it was a fairly amusing situation. I saw no point in acting like a gentleman when Fleet moved toward the bedroom door. She must have been waiting, because the door opened before he could reach it. He stopped. She was wearing my seersucker robe. Her feet were bare. Her hair was neatly combed—as neatly as the curly hairdo would permit. Her face was clean and devoid of makeup, and she looked like a surprisingly nice girl.

"Goody," she said. "Visitors. I'll make some coffee."

Fleet watched her walk past him and into the kitchen. He must have recognized her, but his face showed no expression. "Alibi?" he asked, turning to me.

"Only if she wants to be."

"What time did she get here?"

"I can't seem to remember."

Marge called from the kitchen, "I got here at one o'clock, Lieutenant. That's my Cadillac outside. On a crummy street like this, somebody must have noticed it. What's Paul supposed to have done, anyway?"

I said, "It's a secret, honey. We're supposed to guess." I glanced at him. "You still want me downtown?" He nodded. I said, "Well, I'll get dressed, then."

When I came into the kitchen, shaved and dressed, all three detectives were in the kitchen having coffee with Marge and talking baseball, which was not, however, the subject uppermost in the minds of the two younger men. The dressing gown looked thinner on her than it ever had on me. She handed me a steaming cup of coffee. I drank it down. The police force rose and moved toward the door. I looked down at Marge. Barefooted, she seemed like a smaller girl.

"Thanks," I said in an undertone. "When I find out what for, I'll let you know."

She grinned. "It's on the house, baby."

"Don't stick your neck out too far," I said. "Not for me. Do you want me to see about getting you some clothes if I can?"

She said, "No, I'll call Sadie and have her bring some stuff over in a taxi. She comes at nine." She put a hand on my arm. "Watch your step, baby. It could get rough. Don't trust anybody. Not even me."

I laughed. "I never have, Marge." She turned her face up for a kiss, and I kissed her. Her lips were cool. She must have been a nice kid once. There are some people you put in a special category. They are the people you met too late. I patted her in the appropriate place, and joined the cops who were waiting in the doorway.

Police headquarters is an old, dirty brick building adjoining the new courthouse. We pulled up at a side entrance. Fleet got out with me and sent the other two off with the car. We walked up the steps and down the hall. They still had brass spittoons in the place. Big men in shirt sleeves were carrying paper cups of coffee around. The elevator had a sliding door outside and a kind of brass gate inside built on the same principle as the gates you buy to keep baby from falling downstairs. It closed with a clash and the operator looked at Fleet.

"Down," Fleet said.

I didn't say anything. I was not well acquainted with police headquarters, but I did not think the detective bureau was located in the basement. However, it seemed unlikely that he was lost. I took my pipe out and filled it. He held a match for me.

"Thanks," I said.

"Still guessing?" he asked.

"No," I said. "Just waiting. You'll spring it on me pretty soon. I'm bracing myself."

The elevator stopped. We walked to the right to where two heavy doors blocked the hall. They were the kind of metal and reinforced glass doors that were supposed to keep a fire in one part of the building from spreading to the other parts. Even if the name of the place had not been on the glass, I would have known where I was by the smell as soon as we stepped inside. I took my pipe out of my mouth and dropped it into my jacket pocket. It seemed improper to smoke in the place; besides, the tobacco seemed to have picked up the pervasive odor. It was not quite the same as the odor you met in a hospital.

"Over here," Fleet said.

We went into another room. Everything was white and sterile except for the desk in the corner and the little heap of personal belongings upon it. There were two wheeled tables in the room. One was empty. What lay upon the other was covered with a sheet. I walked over there with Fleet. He turned the sheet back delicately.

I was ashamed of my first reaction; ashamed and surprised. Relief was hardly the proper attitude. The small dead face looked up at me, slack and gray-lipped. One eye was open. You'd have thought they'd have the decency to close them both.

"Recognize her?"

"Yes," I said.

I stood there for a little while in silence, while something changed inside me. I don't know why it should have made a difference. This girl was nothing to me. But it made a difference. No man is an island. Seek not to learn for whom the bell tolls; it tolls for thee. Sentiments courtesy of Donne, via Hemingway.

"Her name's Jeanie," I said. "I never learned the rest."

"You spent the week-end with her?"

"Yes."

"When did you see her last?"

"About six-thirty last night. I drove her to her place and left her there."

"And came home and went out to dinner with another girl? You get around, Mr. Nyquist." There was nothing in that requiring an answer, and I did not speak. He went on: "Would you know any reason why she should be murdered?"

"Was she murdered?"

For answer, he swept the sheet aside. There was no reason why I should have flinched, but I did, although I had seen worse in the war. It reminded me nastily of the small mangled things you see on any highway carrying highspeed traffic.

"Cut it out," I said. It seemed unfair to look at her. She had been kind of a pretty girl. "Cover her up. I'll confess. Just cover her up."

He replaced the sheet. "She was knocked on the head, put into the street, and a car was run over her," he said.

"My car?" I asked.

"Don't you know?"

"No," I said. "It was there when I left the place last night. It was there when I came back. It was there in the morning. I haven't checked the mileage, and couldn't remember the figures if I tried."

"It wasn't your car. Unless you've had it washed, and there's too much dust and dirt on it for that."

I said, "That's the first good argument I've heard for keeping a dirty car."

"You also have an alibi," Fleet said. "I guess that lets you out."

"Was I ever in?"

"Did you quarrel with her on Sunday?"

"No."

"The report I have says she threw a beer at you. You were having a drink with her and another man out on

Smitty's Pier, at Poplar Island. Who was the other man?"

"Jack Williams, reporter for the *Courier*. The beer was thrown at him," I said. "Although it would be a little hard to prove who she was aiming at, I grant you. Pitching wasn't her strong point." There was no reason why I should lie for Jack Williams.

Fleet said, "The girls in her apartment say somebody called her up. She acted snotty to him at first, but softened up. They thought he was apologizing for something, trying to make up after a fight. They assumed it was the person with whom she'd spent the week-end. She agreed to meet him somewhere. They didn't catch the place. She got dressed and went out. It was about ten-thirty. The doctor says she was killed around three. She had been knocked around some before that. There were bruises that had had time to color up before she died. A patrolman found her in an alley on the east side at four thirty-five. Well, come on upstairs and write up a statement for us, and you can go."

When I got home, the place was empty. Marge had left no signs of her presence except the highball glass still standing in its puddle by the living room chair, a wet towel in the bathroom, and some dirty dishes in the kitchen. I shoved bread into the toaster, lit a fire under the remnants of the coffee, and put some water on for eggs.

It was no use calling Marge on the phone, I thought. She had known something was going to happen. She had known I might be needing an alibi, and she had supplied it. If I questioned her about it, she would either lie or tell the truth, and I could guess the truth already. It was better to leave her out of it. I owed her that much.

chapter twelve

HOFFY WAS in the shop when I came down. He had a laminated blank on the bench and was sitting smoking his pipe and looking at it. He would sit there most of the day like that, I knew, just looking at it, like a diamond-cutter studying an important stone. Since there is little grain to worry about in a laminated stock, the performance didn't impress me as much as it might have.

I said, "There's no rush on that bull-gun, Hoffy. Why don't you first finish up the sporter for Mr. Vance and get him off our necks?"

"Why don't you do your work, mine friend, and let me do mine?"

This meant simply that he had just finished working on one light sporter stock and now he wanted to make a heavy target stock. He'd been working in walnut and now he wanted to work in laminated wood, although he usually scorned the stuff and referred to it as plywood. Like I've said, Hoffy's an artist. He watched me take the finished gun from the rack.

"If you'd get up in the morning," he said, "you'd have nice shooting. Now there's a wind."

"Less than eight miles per hour," I said. "At a hundred yards it won't affect this baby a bit."

"Well, don't let her get too hot," he said. "And watch with those screwdrivers, *hein?*"

I said, "Why don't you do your work, Hoffy, and let me do mine?"

He rumbled in his chest, his idea of a chuckle. "She's a pretty gun, Paul. A pretty gun. Let me see her."

I put the weapon in his hands and watched him, an ugly, bristly tub of a man, run his blunt fingers gently along the comb of the stock. It gave me a funny feeling. Hoffy might be a bastard to get along with, but he was not a jerk by my definition of the word, and this made him rare and priceless. Unlike most of the people with whom I'd been associating of late, he wasn't just out for what he could get any way he could get it. He had a code, he had standards, he had a star to steer by. One million dollars cash would not buy from him work that was less than his best: he would destroy it first. I watched him find a rag and wipe an imaginary fingerprint from the satin blue of the barrel.

"A pretty gun," he said. "For a woman who would rather have a fur coat. Who could have been satisfied out of the Sears Roebuck catalog. Here. Take it and get out. I have work to do. Somebody must work in this place."

The Capital City Rod and Gun Club is located about four miles straight out Western Boulevard from the shop, which makes it handy for us. That, although most of the members don't know it, is why it's there. It was a typical Gunderman operation. I happened to mention casually one day that Hoffy and I were having trouble finding a place to test our guns. The National Guard Armory had an indoor range but it wouldn't take the heavy stuff we were firing. We'd made a deal with a farmer, but his neighbors were getting nervous. Carl said for me not to give it another thought.

Two weeks later the Capital City Rod and Gun Club came into existence. The membership list, at fifty bucks a head, looked like a who's who of local politics, and included also just about everybody who did business with either city or state. I never did learn how he leased the land or from whom, but the earthmoving machinery that leveled off the range and shoveled up the twenty-foot back-stop kind of wandered over one day from a nearby highway-construction project. Trucks drifted in and dumped piles of cinder blocks for the club- and trap-houses. Workmen showed up and threw the stuff together and disappeared.

It all took less than a month. Rather to Carl's surprise, the organization turned out to be highly successful and popular. The trapshooting addicts have held several well-attended events each year and will play host to the state shoot this summer. We have a regular series of pistol matches with teams from the police, various reserve organizations, and all the sporting-goods stores in town. In advance of the hunting season we open the range to hunters who want to sight in their guns, and run a course on safety in the woods. I got together with some characters from the YMCA and Boy Scouts and started a junior rifle club which is going strong. Regardless of how it started, the place seems to fill a community need. Meanwhile, Nyquist and Hoffmeyer have a nice hundred-yard range at their disposal. I suppose I could work up some guilt feelings about it if I tried.

There was a light southeasterly breeze and a bright sun. I got the stuff laid out on the table and walked down to tack up the targets. When I started back, there was another car beside the Plymouth: one of those convertibles that don't convert, in two tones of green liberally laced with chrome. I don't suppose he had picked the color to contrast with his hair, but the thought came to mind. You got a very odd slant on people, sometimes, from the cars they picked to drive.

He was standing by the bench-rest, looking down at the gun, when I came up. He still looked like a redheaded farm boy with mail-order glasses. I remembered him dancing with Jeanie at Smitty's Pier. He was studying the gun with a wary look, like a man confronted by a rattlesnake. You can always tell when they don't know anything about it.

I said, "Hi, Jack. How's the column coming?"

He shrugged his shoulders. "That's a nice-looking gun. What caliber is it?"

I said, "It's called .25 Souper. All those wildcat cartridges have fancy names. Souper, Helldiver, Wasp—"

"Wildcat?"

I grinned. "Slang for a privately developed cartridge not commercially manufactured. This one is made from a .308 case necked down to .25 caliber. The .308 is the same as the new experimental Army T-65 cartridge. Now do you know any more than before you asked?"

Jack Williams grinned. I gave him credit for the effort, but the execution was terrible. He looked like a man with a load on his mind. Well, it would come out eventually; meanwhile I kept on talking as I got the scope out of the factory carton and locked it in place on the mount.

"The customer wanted a light mountain rifle for his wife. This is about as light as you can get a bolt-action gun: seven pounds with the scope. It's a twenty-inch Titus barrel on a Mauser action with a full-length Mannlicher-style stock." I pulled the bolt to check the barrel. It was clear. I replaced the bolt, arranged the sandbags, seated myself on the bench, and got the gun into position. I counted five shells out of the box and fed one into the gun. "The scope is a four-power Stith on a Stith adjustable mount," I said. "There are no iron sights because the lady doesn't know how to use them. Hold onto your ears now. It's a little noisy."

The target came up nice and clear in the scope. We shoot at the bench-rest target which has a black box for aiming point instead of the solid round bull. The white center of the box makes it possible to position the crosshairs more accurately. The gun roared and recoiled. The short barrel made for quite a bit of muzzle blast. I opened the bolt and picked out the fired shell, set it aside, and reached for another.

"We save the brass for reloading, of course," I said. "If this were a target rifle I'd warm it up with two or three rounds before firing for record. However, it's slightly impractical to warm up a gun in the field before taking a crack at a charging grizzly, so we sight in our hunting rifles cold, the way they'll be used."

I fired again. It was a good day, and I could see the shots with the four-power scope without referring to the big spotting telescope set up on the table beside me. I gestured toward it.

"Take a look, if you like. Turn the tube to focus."

He cleared his throat, and seemed about to unload the thing that weighed on him, but thought better of it, and crouched down behind the big scope. The two shot holes were within half an inch of each other, but like most laymen he was not impressed. One stray shot in the middle of the bull will have them clapping you on the back and cheering, while a ten-shot group that can be covered by a dime will leave them cold if it happens to be off in a corner of the paper somewhere. They don't seem to realize that the size of the group is the important criterion, both of the gun and of your shooting ability. Once you can put all your bullets through the same hole, you can move that hole around wherever you please—into the middle of the X-ring if you like. That's what sight adjustments are for.

"Are you shooting at that black square?" Jack asked. "You're a little high, aren't you?"

"It's supposed to be high," I said. "Three inches high at a hundred yards. That'll make it about three and a half inches high at a hundred and fifty, about two and three quarters high at two hundred, on the button at two-fifty, and about four inches low at three hundred. Since the lady probably can't hold that close, anyway, particularly when she's puffing and panting from climbing a mountain, it means that she can shoot at any range up to three hundred yards with the same sight setting. Three or four inches one way or another isn't going to make her miss a target the size of a mountain goat."

I fired again, and, at measured intervals, twice more. I never quite trust a three-shot group; it can be a fluke. Even five shots aren't a completely reliable indication of how a gun is behaving, but with a light rifle it's about as long a string as you can put together. I rose and walked down there. Jack came along. I put my pocket ruler across the group and got an inch and a quarter, not spectacular but not bad for a light sporter. The center of the group was about half an inch below where I wanted it. I went back to the table and got out the wrench and brought the elevation up two notches. Then I sat down and got out my pipe and pen-knife.

"Well, now she's got to cool," I said, reaming out the bowl of the pipe. "A light barrel like that gets erratic as hell when it gets hot. What's on your mind, Jack?"

"Did you kill her?" he asked. "Did you kill Jeanie?"

I looked up at him. "No," I said. "You did."

chapter thirteen

HE LOOKED startled first; then he looked shocked; then he began to get angry. I held up my hand quickly when he started to speak.

"Wait a minute," I said. "Suppose you'd walked her up to the edge of the platform and shoved her into the path of the Southland Express, would you blame the train? If you'd pushed her into a cage with a man-eating lion, which you'd first teased into a rage, would it be the lion's fault if he yielded to his natural instincts? You reform characters make me sick sometimes. Why couldn't you leave the kid alone?"

He said, "Well, that's a beautiful bit of sophistry, I must say! So now murder is a natural instinct!"

"Tell me a time when it wasn't."

"Well, I doubt if a jury is going to pay much attention to that argument!"

"Who's talking about juries?" I said. "Anyway, if you're looking at me, you're a damn fool. I'm not a lion or an express train and I didn't kill her. You killed her with your questions and telephone calls. . . . All right, all right. So you didn't hit her over the head with a blackjack and run over her with a car. Somebody else did that. But if you'd let her alone she'd be alive today. That makes you as responsible as anybody else; morally, if not legally. It was you who called her up last night, wasn't it?"

"Yes, but—"

I said, "The pen is mightier than the sword, and that goes for the telephone, too. You've just proved it." I lit my pipe and turned away from him to put the empty shells back into the box.

"If you didn't kill her yourself," he said, "you had her killed. What did you talk to Gunderman about last night? And why should Gunderman's girl give you an alibi? How did you know you were going to need an alibi?"

I asked, "Why should I kill her?"

"Why, to keep her from talking to me, of course."

I said, "Jack, I'm afraid you've got delusions of grandeur. Why the hell should I care what she said to you?"

"It would kind of depend on what she had to say, wouldn't it?" His voice was nasty.

"I can assure you," I said, "that nothing she could have had to say would have made me kill her. Absolutely nothing." I picked five fresh shells from the box and examined the bullets for flaws: sometimes you get one that isn't quite perfect, particularly near the point.

Jack said, "I might believe you if it wasn't for the fact that you'd already committed one murder to cover your trail. You don't think anybody's fooled by that police story about a gun battle in the Wadsworth Building, do you? We have ways of learning things the way they happen. Samuel Banks wasn't killed by any police revolvers, he was practically blasted apart by the bullet from a heavy rifle fired at close range. Why did you kill him, Nyquist? Was he there to make sure you did a good job? Did he threaten you when you lost your nerve and refused to shoot again? Or were you just wiping out a witness against you?"

"Samuel Banks," I said. "Samuel Banks?"

"Better known as Whitey."

"Oh," I said. "That jerk." I grimaced. "Jack, you're covering a lot of territory here. So far, according to you, I have two killings and a near miss to my credit. Where does Jeanie come into the picture?"

"Well, you seem to make a habit of using women for alibis," he said.

"And rubbing them out afterward?" I murmured. "Poor Marge. You'd better warn her she's living on borrowed time."

Jack said, "Jeanie wasn't very happy about the way you'd treated her. She threw out a few hints. I've been doing a little investigating. It seems that there were two men who looked pretty much alike. One drove down to Poplar Island with a girl. The other arrived almost ten hours later by bus. The first man was whisked away and put on a plane, leaving the impression that the second man, who happens to be an expert marksman, had been at Poplar Island the entire afternoon Governor Maney was shot."

I grinned. "Jack, it's a good thing you don't write fiction. This sounds pretty much like the old gag about the twin brother from Australia. Two identical characters—"

"They wouldn't have to be identical. Just the same height and coloring. A man with Carl Gunderman's contacts could pick up somebody for the job easily enough."

"Wait a minute," I said. "Now we've got Carl in on this. Where did he come from?"

"Well, your friendship with Gunderman isn't exactly a secret. And even if you had some personal reason for wishing Governor Maney dead, you'd hardly have the facilities for covering up afterward the way this thing's been covered up."

I set the five shells carefully on their bases in a straight row, like soldiers at attention, and looked up at him. "There's only one thing wrong with your whole argument, Jack," I said. "From anybody else it would sound fine. But from a representative of the *Courier* it stinks. Hell, it's your paper that's been bleating for years that Maney's anti-crime crusade was nothing but a front and that actually he was in league with all the crooks and racketeers in the state, particularly Carl Gunderman. Now you have Gunderman arranging to kill him, if I follow your reasoning correctly."

He said stiffly, "Thieves have been known to fall out before now. Perhaps Maney decided to polish up his record before going into national politics. Maybe he was planning a big cleanup campaign as his last act in office. Gunderman got wind of the double cross. . . ."

"Okay," I said, laughing, "okay, so Carl hired me to knock off Maney. I got buck fever and missed. Whitey got snotty about it, so I bumped off Whitey. Jeanie talked too much so I took care of her. That puts you kind of on the spot, doesn't it, Jack? Aren't you getting a little nervous? Here's a gun handy, and shells, and everything. A nice, lonely place where gunshots are commonplace. . . . What's the matter now?"

A thoughtful look had come into his eyes. "I just thought of something," he said. "What if you didn't miss?"

I said, "You'd better develop that idea a little. I find it hard to grasp in its present form."

"What if you didn't miss?" he repeated. "What if it

happened just the way it was supposed to happen. That would explain everything. What better way for Maney to whitewash himself than for him to be the victim of a murderous attack by...." My laughter stopped him. "Well, it's a possibility," he said, rather sulkily.

"No," I said, chuckling. "It isn't even a possibility. First, can you see Maney letting himself be shot anywhere, even for the sake of his political career? He's ambitious, but not that ambitious. Second, if I were going to shoot him for show—I presume I'm still elected to handle the gun—would I have used a soft-nosed bullet instead of something that would drill a clean hole? Third, I couldn't guarantee to hit a man's arm at four hundred yards, and I don't think there's anybody in the world who could. The man, yes. The arm, no." I tested the barrel of the rifle. It was still too warm. "Jack," I said, "if I were you, I'd lay off. You've already got one person killed, nosing around. Why don't you give it a rest? A hundred years from now you'll be surprised how little difference it'll make." He did not speak. I looked up at him. "You've got your work to do," I said. "You've got to figure the possibilities, I suppose. I'm not sore because you suspect me. I realize it's a kind of intellectual exercise. You've got to suspect everybody. But I'd like to put it to you straight, Jack. We've known each other, off and on, for a couple of years now. You've drunk my liquor and I've drunk yours. In that time you must have formed some kind of an opinion of me. Could you—answer honestly now—could you conscientiously say that I impress you as the sort of guy who'd lie in wait to murder an unarmed and unsuspecting man? Or be party to having a girl beaten and blackjacked and crushed under the wheels of a car?"

It was the old man-to-man approach, putting the whole thing on a personal basis. It was a dirty trick, and I suppose I deserved that it didn't work. He squirmed first, and then he looked me straight in the eye.

"Two days ago," he said, "I'd have answered no to that. Even last night. But this morning, when I heard that Jeanie had been killed...."

He broke off. His voice had changed slightly. I caught on at last. He wasn't here for his paper. He wasn't here for the truth, for society, for posterity, or for his byline in print. He was here for Jack Williams; and he was mad, cold mad, way down inside. That girl—that dumb, pouty little girl—had struck a chord somewhere. He'd had a good time with her, until she tossed a beer in his face for being a reporter. She had clicked; he'd seen something there that he'd been missing a long time—perhaps all his life. Well, I had no business laughing. It had happened to other people. It had happened to me.

"I'll get the man who did it," he said. "I don't care who he is, I'll get him."

I watched him drive off in his fancy car. The gun was cool enough. I slid a shell into the chamber and got back to work.

chapter fourteen

JIM HINES, the kid we'd hired a few weeks ago, was holding down the fort alone when I got back. He was busy fitting a new mainspring to an old Colt Single Action revolver. In my opinion, that gun is the most overrated firearm in history, and I suspect that more cowboys and Indians were killed just from falling off their horses, drunk, than ever fell to the old forty-five. Nevertheless, now that the model is no longer manufactured, every man who owns one is under the illusion that he's the custodian of an irreplaceable treasure, so we keep patching the damn things up as they break down, which happens with monotonous regularity. I laid my gear on the bench and called Jim over. If I'd gone over to him he'd have thought I was trying to coddle him and got mad. One thing we had plenty of in the place was temperament.

He found his crutches and swung himself across the shop toward me. Polio had hit him at the age of ten or thereabouts. Despite his handicap, the kid was an excellent, careful workman and loved guns and could shoot like a machine from any position he was capable of assuming. He had even taught himself to shoot standing, but of course it wasn't legal for competition because of the crutches. Prone or from a bench rest he was right in there with the good ones and had the medals to prove it.

"Where's Hoffy?" I asked.

"He went out for a beer," Jim said, and grinned, and

waved his hand toward the laminated blank still resting, untouched, on Hoffy's bench. "Got tired of staring at it, I guess. Couldn't seem to visualize it right, or something. He's a screwball, isn't he?"

"Yes," I said, a little shortly. The place was crawling with screwballs. When you came right down to it, all this business with guns was undoubtedly a form of psychological compensation for all of us. Just a bunch of frustrated screwballs sublimating our aggressive impulses in the fabrication of instruments of death. I could sling the lingo, too. God knows I had been exposed to enough of it. I pulled the .25 rifle out of the case. "This baby's ready to go," I said to Jim. "Grease her good and wrap her up and have Railway Express come get her. Before you seal the package, make damn sure you put in the Allen wrench for the scope. The address is in the file. Okay?"

"Check, Mr. Nyquist. What about shells?"

"There's a hundred rounds of the 117-grain loads all made up. Send them separately. You can stick this target in with them." I wrote the loading data on the target, stamped it TESTED BY, and wrote my initials after the stamp. "Anything come in I should know about?"

"A man brought in a Model 70 Hornet he wants rechambered to .222 Remington."

"Want to take a crack at it?" I asked.

"Sure." He tried not to sound eager. It was the biggest job he had been given so far.

"Okay. Well, I'm going around the corner to get something to eat. If Hoffy comes in, tell him I said to quit staring and start whittling."

I had not really noticed that the day was getting hot until I stepped into the restaurant and the air conditioning hit my damp shirt. It took me a while to dry off and get comfortable in the artificial climate. I didn't pay much attention to the food; in there it was never anything to get excited about. When I came out on the street again, the heat and light seemed to strike me in the face. I turned back toward the shop. Suddenly there was a man on either side of me, falling into step with me.

"The big guy wants to see you," one of them said.

They were both jerks. Their faces were vaguely familiar; I had seen them around; but to me they were all jerks and I never bothered to learn their names. Despite the heat they were wearing their suit coats.

I said, "Okay, but let me stop by the place for a minute—"

"Now," the jerk said.

I kept walking between them. We were getting close. "What's the rush?" I asked reasonably. "I just want to tell the boy—"

"Write him a letter," the jerk said, and caught my arm. I swung with the pull, so that his own effort threw him off balance; I took a step forward and caught the lapels of his coat and pulled the coat off his shoulders and down around his elbows, locking his arms; at the same time swinging him around. The swing gave him lots of momentum. I put him like a shot right into the arms of jerk number two, and they both went down. Then I was inside the shop.

There was a rack of guns, for show, just inside the door. I grabbed the most lethal-looking of the bunch, a big old outside-hammer ten-gauge double gun. As far as I knew there wasn't a ten-gauge shell within two miles of us, but the big hammers sounded dangerous as hell when I hauled them back to full cock and stepped back into the doorway. The gun was a real old-timer, with Damascus barrels: in those days they hadn't licked the problem of making solid steel barrels for shotguns, so they wrapped strips of steel spirally around a rod and soldered them together to form a tube. The result was strong enough for the old black-powder loads, but I wouldn't have fired modern ammunition through that gun for a million dollars.

The jerks on the sidewalk didn't know the difference. All they could see were the big twin bores and the cocked hammers. They froze in the act of picking themselves up. One of them—the one who was still wearing his coat in a proper fashion—eased his hand back into sight, empty.

I said, "Tell him if he wants me he can call me up and ask me. Maybe I'll come, if I'm not too busy."

They dusted themselves off and went away. I lowered the hammers of the antique and hung it back on the wall, and looked around quickly at a sound. Jim Hines was easing a shell out of the chamber of the .25 Souper he had been preparing for shipment. He looked up, and grinned.

"Is this a private fight?" he asked. "Or can anybody join?"

"Fight?" I said. "Who's fighting? This is just a comedy

routine, kid. Don't take it seriously." I looked at him for a moment longer. "I mean that."

"Okay, boss."

The telephone started to ring. They must have stopped right around the corner to make their call. I picked up the instrument, and heard Carl Gunderman's voice.

"Getting tough as hell these days, aren't you, boy?"

"Keep your tame creeps at home," I said. "Next time I'll really scare them. I'll put shells in the gun, and everything."

I heard him burst out laughing. "You mean the cannon was empty? Wait till they hear that!" Then he stopped laughing. "What about dropping over to the house for a couple of minutes, Paul? Or do I have to say please?"

"I think I can make it," I said.

"You bastard," he said fondly. "One of these days one of the boys is going to get sore and blow your head off."

I said, "You mean he'll try. I'll see you, Carl." I hung up the phone and looked at Jim and grinned. "Like I said. Just a routine to amuse the customers. Keep your nose clean. I'll be back some time."

Carl had bought himself the house out in Wendover Hills the year before. It was quite an establishment, and I always felt disrespectful driving up in a cheezy little Plymouth. Carl himself had suggested that he would appreciate my washing the car if I was going to park it in his drive very often, which was another good reason for leaving it dirty. He was getting to be hell on appearances, these days. In a way it was reassuring that he had asked me to the house instead of the office, since he did not usually let the jerks hang around the house.

He was waiting out front for me, holding down one of half a dozen rustic chairs that surrounded a large redwood table that in turn supported a beach umbrella. He was wearing a sports shirt decorated with palm leaves, light slacks, and the kind of moccasin shoes known as loafers. Brooks was with him. Brooks was a tall enough man, but he looked like a toothpick beside the big boy. They both watched me drive up. I got out of the car and walked across the lawn.

"Pour the boy a drink, Brooks," Carl said. "Then get somebody to for Christ's sake drive that wreck out of my front yard."

"No drink," I said.

"Pay no attention to him, Brooksie," Carl said. "He's just feeling negative today."

"No drink," I said. Brooks looked at Carl, got a nod and walked off.

"What's the matter with you, anyway?" Carl asked me. "You're getting harder to get along with than a porcupine or something. Are you mad about something, boy?"

I looked at him for a moment, but all I could see was the crushed body of a girl on a white table. He looked at me and grinned. He knew what I was thinking. I had thrown him a challenge last night. I had told him to lay off Williams. He had laid off Williams, all right. Well, it was too late or too early to do anything about that. I looked around.

"Where's Marge?" I asked.

"Marge went away," Carl said. I looked at him quickly. He said, "Far away. I don't like my friends playing games behind my back, boy."

I said carefully, "Why, Carl, I didn't think you'd be jealous."

He grinned. "She should have had sense enough not to mix into business. When I want you to have an alibi, boy, I'll give you an alibi."

I said, "I kind of liked Marge."

"Maybe that's why I sent her away. Don't do anything rash, pal. I kind of liked Marge myself. I wouldn't hurt her."

"Okay," I said. "Okay."

"She's just taking a little vacation," Carl said. "It was about time, anyway. Can't have a woman thinking she owns you. Why the kid was beginning to talk marriage. You're spreading yourself kind of thin, aren't you, Paul? First Williams and now Marge. You've got a lot of credit with me, you know that, but don't try to stretch it to cover all your friends."

"I'll keep it in mind," I said. "I'll certainly keep it in mind."

"You bastard," he said. "You don't give a damn, do you? It's just a game to you. Well, it isn't a game to me, see? Don't get in my way, Paul. I know where I'm going, and I'll run over you or anybody else to get there."

"Sure," I said.

"I've done a lot for you, since you came here. I've given you a hand all the way. And that's the way it should be.

I pay my debts, boy. But there's a limit, see? What did Williams want with you today? What's with you and Williams anyway?"

I said, "He wanted to know if I'd killed that girl, Jeanie."

Carl threw back his head and roared with laughter. "And that's the guy you've been standing up for!"

"Uhuh," I said. "And it still goes. Leave him alone."

"He's getting too damn nosy. He's getting too damn close—"

I said, "He's not even in the same county with the truth, Carl. He thinks you wanted Maney killed because he was double-crossing you in some way. How much harm can anybody do, thinking that? It's what you want him to think, isn't it?"

"Well," Carl said. "Maybe. But why do you care what happens to him?"

I said, "He's a man doing a job. He's got ideals. I'm sentimental. I want him left alone."

Carl said, "Maybe. But don't get too damn sentimental, my friend. Don't get too palsy-walsy with Williams or any other reporter, see? I still don't like the looks of that loused-up operation Saturday. If I thought you were playing games with me; if I thought you'd muffed that shot on purpose—" He drank from his glass, and set it back on the table. "Brooks thinks you're playing games."

"I lie awake every night worrying about what Brooks thinks."

"Brooks has a head on his shoulders."

"He'd look funny as hell without one."

Carl glanced at me, and said in a casual voice, "Who was the girl, Paul?"

"What girl?"

"The girl who helped you make your getaway Saturday." He held up his hand. "Wait a minute, boy. I'll play this straight, for old times sake. No traps, no nothing. Cards on the table." He raised his voice. "Hey, Brooks!"

There was a sound, and Brooks stepped out of the bushes. There was a jerk with him. They come and they go. I'd never seen this one before.

Brooks said to the jerk, "Okay. Spill it."

The jerk said, "Well, I seen him come around the corner of the building—"

"What building?" Brooks asked.

"The Wadsworth Building. The one I was supposed to be

watching. What the hell do you think? I could see him plain through the glasses. He was carrying some kind of a trumpet case. The dame was all loaded down with packages like she'd been shopping—"

"What did she look like?"

"Not bad, except for the cheaters. Blue suit and hat. Five-five or six. I said she was wearing glasses, didn't I? They came up the street and ducked into O'Hearn's parking lot and I lost them."

Carl said, "Why didn't you mention this before, stupid?"

"Nobody asked me. I mean, I knew he was supposed to have a girl for an alibi and I figured it was the same girl."

Carl said, "Next time, don't figure. Okay, get back downtown." The jerk moved off. Brooks stood there, watching me and hoping. Carl said, "This was around three on Saturday, boy. The Jeanie kid was down at Poplar Island by that time, with your double. So it wasn't her. Marge was with me. So it wasn't her. Let's hear you talk."

I shrugged. "What's there to say? I left myself an out, that's all. In case something should go wrong. It did." I hoped my voice sounded easy and convincing.

"About this out. Let's hear more about her."

"Just a girl I know. I had her standing by with a car and money, just in case. It had occurred to me that you might decide to sell me out, Carl. I apologize for the thought."

"Apologies are fine but I like names better."

I said, "No names, Carl."

"Why not? Don't you trust me, boy?"

"Hell, no," I said. "Not with somebody else's life. Just with my own."

Brooks said, "Let me try. I can get it out of him."

Carl opened his mouth to speak, and closed it again, as a car turned into the drive below us. It took a while to come into sight.

Carl said quickly, "If this is who I think it is, you're both going to be nice. Real nice."

He got up, and brushed off his slacks, and ran a hand over his hair. The approaching car came up the drive fast and skidded to a stop in the white gravel. It was a red-and-cream Buick convertible; the sporter model with the overgrown rear fenders. The top was down. The girl at the wheel was blonde and wore a white suit. She got out gracefully, without displaying any more leg than necessary. The jerk who played butler was holding the car door for her; he bowed the way he had seen it done in a movie and pointed us out to her.

Carl said softly, "How do you like that for class, eh? Be nice, now."

He went forward to meet her. Brooks and I followed. Carl took the girl's hand. She had a nice, cultured voice.

"I do hope I'm not early. I got hungry."

Carl said, "No. Some business came up, but we're all through. You've met Mr. Brooks, my business partner. And this is Paul Nyquist, a friend. Paul, Carla McMahon."

The girl shook hands with me. We talked about the weather for a few minutes, all four of us. We'd had a cool spring but it looked as if we were going to make up for it now. The girl made her contributions to the conversation like a well-brought-up young lady. You could see that she knew precisely who she was and who we were, and she was wondering just where we packed our guns, and it was all very exciting to be standing there with us talking about the weather. She had never known any gangsters before. She wouldn't have missed it for the world.

Brooks took his cue from Carl. "Well, I've got to be getting back downtown."

I said, "Well, I guess I'd better run along, too." I bowed to Miss McMahon, and turned away.

Carl's voice said, "Paul. Just a minute. . . . Excuse me, Carla." I stopped and waited for him. He put his hand on my arm. "About that girl, Paul. Can she keep her mouth shut?"

"Yes."

"She'd better," he said. "You tell her."

"I'll tell her," I said. "Have a good time."

chapter fifteen

WENDOVER HILLS was far enough from town to give me time for some thinking on the way back. My thinking revolved mainly about two girls, one of whom I had last seen on a slab in the morgue. It seemed very likely that the other was heading the same way, despite the reassuring note upon which I had parted from Carl. Even if he had been sincere, which was doubtful, he would change his mind; or Brooks would change it for him. Brooks was a great boy for direct action.

I was rolling along at an easy thirty-five when a police car pulled up alongside and signaled me to the curb. The cops were quite polite.

"Mr. Nyquist? Mr. Paul Nyquist?"

"That's right," I said.

"Lieutenant Fleet would like to see you, sir."

"Where?"

"Down at Headquarters."

One advantage of having an official escort was that I had no trouble parking—although I didn't put it past them to have a ticket on the car when I came out. Fleet's office was on the third floor. He got up and shook hands and moved a chair an inch or so and asked me to sit down. I sat down. I refused a cigarette and loaded my pipe. He was ready with a match, sitting on the edge of the desk above me. He grinned abruptly, cracking the impassive layers of his face.

"This is a pretty good treatment, eh?" he said. "Makes people nervous as hell to have cops be nice to them."

I said, "I'm looking for the gimmick."

"Had a reporter in here," he said. "Fellow from the *Courier*."

"Williams."

"That's right. Jack Williams. He's a fast boy with a theory. He's got it all figured out. About that girl that was killed last night. About Governor Maney being shot."

"I know," I said. "He told me. While I was sitting in front of him with a loaded rifle. Some people don't care where they die."

"Where were you Saturday?"

"What time Saturday?"

"All day."

"Apartment until about nine a.m.," I said. "Did some work in the shop until ten-thirty. Got in the car and picked up the kid at her place. I wanted to start earlier but she liked to sleep late."

"She's sleeping late now," Fleet said.

I said, "Yes. We got started about eleven, I think. Had lunch at some joint on the way down—"

"Remember the place?"

"No," I said. "It wasn't worth remembering. They had those prefabricated hamburgers made out of old rubber boots. Wait a minute. It was called Chick's Drive-in. We got down to the Island around two-thirty, I'd say. Checked in at the Rainbow Court. The kid was in a bad mood. Didn't want to do anything. Had a hangover. The cabin had air conditioning, so we just loafed around and sampled the bottle. Didn't get out to eat until after nine. Got back some time after midnight. Do you want Sunday, too?" With a little practice I might get to be a pretty good liar.

"No," he said. "That's enough. What about the other guy?"

"What other guy?" I grinned. "Oh, you mean Williams's brainwave? My double? Why, Lieutenant, if you find him you can have him."

He grinned back at me. "If I find him, I can have you, you mean."

"Yes," I said. "But for what?"

"Somebody shot Governor Maney on Saturday afternoon. Or had you forgotten?"

I said, "I still want to hear the charge. What's the penalty for shooting a governor in the arm?"

"Assault with intent to kill—"

"Now, wait a minute," I said. "Just wait a minute, Lieutenant. You'd have to prove the intent part, wouldn't you? Didn't Jack Williams tell you the rest of his theory? According to him I shot Governor Maney through the arm with full permission and encouragement from Maney himself. It was a publicity stunt, according to Jack. To counteract the underhanded sniping of certain local newspapers. To offset the exposés they were promising to spring this fall. To boost the governor's campaign for the Senate. To demonstrate the bitter enmity he has earned from the criminal element of the state as a result of his untiring efforts—" Fleet made a sound. I said, "Why, Lieutenant!"

Fleet was watching me closely. "Williams didn't mention this part of his theory."

I said, "I laughed him out of it, as a matter of fact. Just between you and me, if there's anybody who can hit a man's arm at four hundred odd yards, he's a better shot than I am. But it makes a good story just the same."

"Oh."

I sucked at my pipe. "In fact," I said, "I think I'll use it if I should be arrested. It sounds like a damn good idea; I'll buy Jack a pencil-sharpener for suggesting it. Simpler than proving I wasn't there. After all, I don't think there's any law against shooting a man in the arm if he asks you to. Which would make me liable only to a fine for discharging firearms within the city limits."

Fleet said, "Of course, the Governor's testimony—"

I looked up at him. "Don't be silly, Lieutenant. Do you think Maney would ever let me be put in a position where I had to use that defense, if he could help it? No matter how screwy it sounds, it would ruin him. After all, there have been hints of him and Gunderman playing ball behind the scenes, and I'm known to be a good friend of Gunderman's—just the guy who'd be elected to sprinkle a few accurate bullets around. Some people would believe the yarn. Enough to make the difference in a close election."

Fleet asked dryly, "And the girl? I suppose she asked you to run a car over her, first knocking herself on the head so it wouldn't hurt?"

I shook my head. "Let's not kid about that," I said. "Maney's arm, okay. I'll make jokes about Maney's arm all day." He was silent. After a while he found a cigar, bit the end off, and lit it. We smoked for a while. At last I said, "You know the answer to that, don't you?"

He nodded. "A couple of goons. Maybe we'll get them and maybe we won't. If we get them, maybe we'll convict and maybe we won't. We found the car. It was stolen earlier in the evening. The tire treads match the marks on her dress. The blood types match. No doubt about the car. And if this were some other country, I know about six characters I'd line up against a wall and use for submachine-gun practice. When they were all dead, I'd know I had the two or three who beat up the girl and killed her. Nobody'd miss the others, either. But I still wouldn't have the guy who gave the orders." After a while, he said, "You've got some nice friends, Nyquist."

"A man can't always pick his friends."

"What have you got on him?"

"What do you mean?" I asked.

"Or has he got it on you?"

I said, "You're too subtle for me, Lieutenant. Spell it out."

"You came to this city about two years ago. Nobody'd heard of you before. One day here you are, opening up a gunsmithing business, and the word goes out the big boy wants to see you get along. No trouble about licenses, building inspectors, nothing. You want a rifle range, he starts a gun club for you. Naturally, we draw certain conclusions."

"Naturally," I said. "But they were wrong."

"Yes," he said. "To the best of my knowledge, they were wrong. No illegal firearms of any kind have ever been traced to you. All our investigations indicate that you run a legitimate, high-class business. In fact, some of the finest rifles in the country are supposed to come from your shop. Furthermore, Major Smith, who runs the Boy Scouts, has nothing but praise for you. Mr. Clendening of the YMCA says you've done wonders with his bunch of dead-end kids, and my sister's oldest boy thinks you're the nuts. On the other hand, you're a bosom pal of the dirtiest crook and racketeer in the state. He buys you a car for a Christmas present."

I said, "Are you expounding a theory here or just fishing for one, Lieutenant? In either case, you're wasting your time." I rose. "Was there anything else you wanted, Lieutenant?"

Fleet said quietly, "It used to be that a man with a badge was known as a peace officer. To me that has always sounded better than the other title, officer of the law. All kinds of people get elected and they pass all kinds of laws. We can't enforce all of them. Some of them we aren't even supposed to enforce. They're just for show. That leaves us one job we can do, and that is to keep the peace. Keep the streets safe so that people can walk them without danger. When the times comes that any one man endangers the peace of the community, we take care of him. One way or another."

I said, "I suppose the lecture has a personal application?"

"Yes. I don't know how you fit into this, Nyquist. You seem to be a nice enough young fellow. My advice to you is to pull out if you can."

I said, "In other words, Maney has given the word, and you can go to work now."

He did not let it bother him, but grinned. "We take what opportunities we get and don't ask questions. Sometimes we have to mark time; sometimes we can go wide open. It's wide open now. You can pass the news along to your friends."

I said, "If you want them scared, scare them yourself, Lieutenant. Incidentally, is there any objection to my leaving town for a day or two? Only for a day or two."

"Where were you thinking of going?"

"The western part of the state. To hunt woodchucks and do some thinking."

He said, "Just so you stick to woodchucks." He paused. "Incidentally, did you ever hear of a man named August, Tony August?"

"Sure," I said. "He had a brother named Pietro, didn't he? It was in the papers."

"Yes. Pete found his girl with another man and did a little carving on both of them with a knife he carried. The defense tried to claim the unwritten law or something; but Pete's carving was too fancy for the jury, and the Governor refused a pardon. Tony was quite upset. Witnesses heard him threaten to take it out on the Governor's hide if Pete burned. Pete burned anyway. Now Tony's missing. We have found evidence that he bought a Springfield rifle a few weeks ago; also a telescopic sight. Would you say it could add up?"

"Maybe," I said. "I'm surprised that he even managed to wing his man, though. None of those pool-room characters can shoot worth a damn. It must have been his lucky day."

"It looks as if he headed for Mexico," Fleet said. "We're working out the rail. We'll get him."

I said, "Hell, and here I thought I was about to be arrested, myself. You cops are too much for me. Can I go now?"

He nodded, and I started to turn away, but checked myself, catching sight of something on the desk. I stepped closer and picked it up. It was a photograph of Jeanie lying dead, not in the morgue downstairs but in the alley where she had been found, before they had got the clothes and dirt and blood off her and made her into a numbered exhibit instead of a dead girl. I looked at it for a moment.

"Do you have an extra copy?" I asked.

"What do you want it for?"

"I'm making a collection," I said.

"You're bad luck·for women, it seems," Fleet said. "I understand your alibi of last night got her walking papers from the big guy. Five thousand cash and a ticket to Chicago."

So that's where Marge had gone. I was relieved to hear it. "News gets around," I said. "What about the picture?"

"Take it. We've got others. But—"

"But what?" I looked at him and grinned. "Oh, be your age, Lieutenant. I haven't the faintest intention of taking the law into my own hands."

Outside, the heat was still building up. The Plymouth was an oven. The apartment, right under the tin roof of the building, was worse. I changed my clothes, got Whitey's P-38 and the .222 woodchuck gun from the rack and cased them; and dragged all the gear down to the car, perspiring freely. The shop was still reasonably cool when I came in, but Hoffy warmed it up some when he heard that I was taking off. Then I was on the dual-lane highway heading west. After a while I let in the overdrive; I usually leave it locked out around town. At seventy the car was nervous. I remembered being advised to balance the wheels. At seventy-five things started fluttering and dancing around in back. The car in the rear-view mirror hung on without effort a couple of hundred yards astern. One thing those jerks can do is drive. I let the speedometer slide back to fifty. Even knowing the back roads as I did, it took me an hour to lose them and make sure they stayed lost.

Two hours and some seventy miles after that I drove into Staley, which is the county seat of Meningo County. The courthouse, fortunately, was still open. I transacted my business, and was told that I would have to wait twenty-four hours, which I already knew from past experience. I could have accomplished the same thing back home, of course. When I was in Fleet's office it would have just been a step down the hall. But too many of the lads in that place draw salaries from two or three sources, and pass out information accordingly.

The next day I hunted woodchucks and had a good time. I don't know why it is that you never appreciate nature quite as much as when you're lying around waiting to shoot something. Very few of the nature-lovers that I know—who are always shocked at the idea of killing little birds and animals—know half as much about nature as I do. They can't be bothered to sit still long enough to learn. Well, I guess it's all in the point of view.

I also did a little shooting with the P-38, since I don't like to carry a gun around without knowing where it's sighted to hit. At four o'clock I dropped by the courthouse; then I got back into the Plymouth and headed south.

chapter sixteen

THE NAME on the mailbox was Powers—R. D. Powers, RFD 3, Box 47. The lettering had been stenciled afresh this spring; it was nice and clear in the early morning sunshine. The mailbox was not new, but it was preserved by a coat of white paint, neatly applied. It was solidly fastened to a straight cedar post. The farm buildings, a quarter mile off the road, looked similarly well cared for. Now that I was here, it seemed a foolish errand. Well, I had been in worse places for less reason.

When I drove in, kids seemed to pop out of the landscape like ants out of a log. The big ones reached for the little ones and hauled them out of the road. I stopped the car in the dust of the yard. There was the usual farm smell of manure and hay and chickens. The kids kind of swarmed into a clump like bees, watching me warily; there were five of them, ranging in stairstep fashion from ten to about three. I'm never much good at guessing babies' ages, never having had any around to practice on.

I said, "This is where Mrs. Wallace lives, isn't it? Is she home?"

The oldest, a boy, turned and yelled, "Babs. Hey, Babs, there's a man to see you."

The next in line, a girl, said scornfully, "She's gone to town, stupid. Can't you see the car's gone?" She turned to me. "She's gone to town, Mister."

A middle-aged woman came out of the house, wiping her hands on an apron. She was sunburned and strongly built and there was no gray in her dark hair. She wore gold-rimmed glasses. Weak eyes seemed to run in the family. I noticed that the girl who had spoken—the two youngest were also girls—had small, horn-rimmed glasses perched on her childish nose. The woman looked at me, and at the door of the car. I saw her expression change when she read the name. It looked as if Sis hadn't kept her mouth completely shut, after all.

"What do you want?"

"I'd like to talk to Mrs. Wallace."

"She's gone to town. I don't know when she'll be back."

"I'll wait," I said.

The woman looked at me. There was fear in her eyes; mostly, I suppose, for the kids. I didn't like it but there was nothing I could do about it except keep talking.

"There's nothing to worry about," I said. "I just want to talk to her."

The woman looked at me a little longer. At last she moved her shoulders jerkily. "All right. She'll be home pretty soon. She just went down to pick up some Cokes and stuff for the kids. It's been so hot they've cleaned us out. Do you want to come inside—"

"Mom," the oldest boy cried excitedly, "Mom, he's got a gun in the car! Mister, what kind of a gun is that?"

When you live and work with guns, you tend to forget how upset the ordinary citizen gets at the sight of a firearm. Johnny's undoubtedly going to be drafted; world conditions being what they are, his life may quite possibly one day depend on his skill with weapons; but we mustn't for God's sake let him be contaminated by one of the nasty things before he gets into uniform. I saw Mrs. Powers's face become pale.

I said, "It's just a kind of a .22, Mrs. Powers. Guns are my business and kind of a hobby, as well." I stepped to the car and pulled out the woodchuck rifle. "You see? My partner made the stock. It's kind of a show piece."

"Does it shoot, Mister?"

She snapped at the boy, "Malcolm! Be quiet!"

I said, "Sure it shoots. Get the shells out of the car and I'll show you." I turned to the girl with the glasses. "Honey, you take that piece of tin over there and set it up against that fence post." I looked at the woman. "Just a little trick shooting, Mrs. Powers. You don't mind?"

She took it as a threat; a display of force, so to speak. I could see her debating the problem in her mind. Her husband was off somewhere. There was a phone in the house, but the police were far away. There was probably a shotgun in the house—most farms had one—but even assuming she could get to it, she couldn't depend on the children getting out of the way if she tried to use it.

I said, "Okay, you kids get back now. Stand clear back of me."

I pushed five shells into the magazine and brought the gun up. It was the first time I had tried it with a .222 and a ten-power scope; the bolt-action slowed me down. For a real show, you need a .22 automatic that'll hold a lot of shells and pump them out fast. But I managed all right. They watched the holes appear in the tin. The smallest child experimented with the sound, covering her ears for one shot, and leaving them uncovered for the next, and laughing.

"It's a man," said the oldest boy.

"I think it's a boat," said the girl.

The younger boy said, "It isn't a boat, either. It's a Ninjun."

It took a while, since I had to keep reloading the five-shot magazine; it also took all the shells I had brought with me.

"It is too a Ninjun," the younger boy said. "Look at his feathers." They all agreed, now, that it was a pretty good Indian.

"Shoot something else," the older boy said. "Shoot that bottle down there."

"I can't," I said. "I haven't any more cartridges. Here, you put the gun back in the car, will you? Watch out, the barrel's hot. And I'd appreciate it if the rest of you kids would pick up all the empty shells you can find and stick them back into the boxes for me so I can load them again some time. Meanwhile maybe I can talk your mother into getting me something to drink."

She walked to the house with me. It seemed dark and cool in the kitchen in comparison with the heat and sunlight outside. I heard her laugh abruptly.

"No more cartridges, eh?"

"Not for that gun. I've got a pistol locked in the glove compartment with a couple of boxes of extra shells."

"I've got a shotgun over the mantelpiece and half a box of duck loads my husband had left over from hunting season."

"Get it," I said, "if it'll make you feel better."

"Barbara said you were a peculiar one. We've got water, milk, and beer."

"It's too early for beer," I said. "Milk's fine."

She filled a glass and gave it to me. "Sit down."

"What did your sister tell you?" I asked, sitting down.

"Everything, I suppose."

I said, "No. Just everything she knew. Which wasn't much. Keep that in mind, Mrs. Powers. She heard a shot and saw two men and a gun in a room. That's the significant evidence. Later she heard a radio report and put two and two together. The answer she got makes me out a very unpleasant character. Nevertheless, she seems to have followed most of my instructions. She didn't turn me in to the police. She must have had some doubts about her own conclusions."

"You did save her life from that other man," Mrs. Powers said. "Also, you let her go. And Governor Maney's alive and doing well, the paper says. We don't know much about politics down here. It seemed . . . it seemed kind of unnecessary to make trouble." She was a little shamefaced about it. They had not done their duty as citizens. "Well," she said honestly, "we were kind of scared to get mixed up in anything like that, to tell you the truth."

I said, "Sometimes it's smart to be scared."

She looked at me for a moment. "Is anything wrong now? Why did you come here?"

I said, "Yes, something's wrong. We were seen leaving. She was seen. They haven't identified her yet, or traced her here, but I'm afraid it's only a matter of time."

"The police?"

I shook my head. "I'm not worrying about the police. Besides, they're mostly barking down another trail."

She hesitated. "Are you here for her sake, or for your own? To shut her up before she can talk against you?"

I said, "Mrs. Powers, if I wanted her shut up, I could have saved myself a long drive. There'll be people coming to shut her up one way or another, as soon as they can find the right address. I wouldn't have had to lift a finger, if that was what I wanted."

"Of course, that's just your word. The word of a hired killer."

She was beginning to feel safe with me now; safe enough to call me names. I grinned. The sound of an approaching car broke up the conversation. I put my empty glass on the table. We listened to the car pull up in the yard, and heard the shrill voices of the kids. Whatever they told her brought her running toward the house. She flung the door open.

"Charlotte!" she cried breathlessly. "Lottie! Are you all

right? What—" Then she saw the two of us sitting there. "Oh!"

The screen door closed behind her. She stood there a moment, silhouetted against the light outside. She was wearing loafers, jeans rolled just below the knee, and one of those white halter or dickey things that look like a regular shirt with the sleeves and back missing. Her shoulders were quite brown. Her dark hair was pulled back and tied into a horsetail effect. She looked too young ever to have been married, let alone to a man who must have been dead at least three years.

"What do you want?" she demanded.

I said, "Do you know how to shoot a pistol?"

"What?"

"I brought you one," I said. "It may come in handy. Come on outside and I'll show you how it works. Not that it'll do much good. It takes about five thousand rounds to make just a passable pistol shot."

chapter seventeen

I WENT over to the station wagon to get the gun. She waited by the kitchen door until I returned. The sister herded the kids away when they tried to follow.

I said, "Your sister's got quite a family there."

"Yes," she said, "Yes, aren't they darlings?"

"Where's her husband?"

"Dick went off to give somebody a hand with something or other. Everybody kind of works on everybody's place around here."

I said, "Look, if you're saying your prayers, don't. I'm not luring you away from the house to murder you."

She glanced at me quickly; then she smiled. "Was I acting like that?"

"Kind of."

"Well," she said, "you must admit it's kind of an unusual situation, Mr. Nyquist."

"Unusual is the word," I said. "Well, this looks like a pretty good place. That bank will act as backstop. Wait right here." I paced off ten yards and set up the empty beer case I had picked up, for a target, and came back to her. "A pistol," I said, "is just about the most ineffectual firearm developed by man. It has very little power and only a genius can shoot one straight. A good rule for a beginner is: if you can't spit on it, don't bother to try to shoot it. Here. Take a crack at it."

I put the gun into her hands. She was reluctant. "But—"

"Use both hands," I said. "The first shot will come hard because the trigger has to cock the hammer. All subsequent ones will come easily because the hammer will be cocked for you by the recoil. Use both hands and keep both eyes open. Fire the whole clip. I've got plenty of extra shells."

"But I—" She sighed. "Oh, all right." She shoved the gun out ahead of her and hauled away at the trigger. The gun crashed and almost jumped out of her hands.

"Go on!" I said sharply. "Keep firing."

She touched the trigger again. Cocked now, the pistol discharged instantly; startled, she tried to control it and set it off again. I saw her jaw tighten. She took a long breath, gripped the gun hard, and got the remaining five shots off in good order. I took the weapon from her hand; and we walked forward to examine the result. There was one hole reasonably centered in the cardboard carton. A second bullet had ripped the edge. I got out a pencil and marked the places. We returned to the firing point.

"Okay," I said. "Try it again."

"Let me see you do it," she said.

I grinned. "Nothing I like better than showing off, Mrs. Wallace." I aimed and fired. "The upper loop of the B in Beer," I said. She went down and came back. "Okay?" I asked.

"Okay," she said. "Well, if you can do it, I can."

"When you've been shooting for twenty years," I said. "All right, stop stalling and get to work. And remember one thing. You don't have to be able to knock the ash from a cigarette at fifty yards. All you really need is to know how to make the thing go boom, and show that you're just aching to start shooting. They aren't going to ask you to show your Expert qualification. A wild woman with a gun will scare anybody. Nobody wants a 9-millimeter slug through the guts, even if it got there by accident."

"Aren't you—" She hesitated. "Aren't you being a little melodramatic, Mr. Nyquist?"

"Uhuh," I said. "Remember Whitey? He was melodramatic as hell, wasn't he?"

She frowned. "But I really don't understand. Why should you. . . . I mean, apparently the people you expect to . . . to try to silence me are your associates; the same people who hired you to kill—"

I saw no point in explaining the situation, or proclaiming my innocence of homicidal intentions. The less she knew, the safer she was.

I said, "Nobody hired me. It was a friendship job, Mrs. Wallace. A friend of mine wanted some shooting done. Shooting and guns are my business. He's done favors for me; I was willing to do a favor for him. That doesn't mean I'm with him all the way."

She said stiffly, "That would be Gunderman, wouldn't it?"

I said, "You do too much guessing, kid. And don't talk about Gunderman in that tone of voice. He's just a man like any other. A little bigger than some, maybe, but just a man. Not the devil. Come on, let's continue the exercise. To load, you push this button and pull the clip out. . . ."

When we came back into the yard, the heat was getting pretty fierce. The wind had dropped, and a corner of a thunderstorm was peeking over the horizon to the west. I stopped halfway to the kitchen door.

"If you'd come to the car," I said, "there's something I'd like to show you."

She hesitated, and nodded. We walked across the yard, kicking up the dust in little spurts.

"Get in," I said. "Make yourself comfortable." She got in, moving a little reluctantly; she still did not trust me a bit. I walked around the other side and got behind the wheel. I laid the P-38 on her lap. "You can point this at me, if it'll make you relax. It's loaded. All you have to do is pull."

"Oh, don't be silly," she said impatiently.

I looked around to make sure the kids weren't going to barge in on us. The sister had them corralled somewhere; they were not in sight. Then I unlocked the glove compartment and took out two separate papers. One was rolled into a cylinder, held by a rubber band. I passed it to her.

"Exhibit One," I said.

She stripped the rubber band off, glanced at me, and unrolled the picture Lieutenant Fleet had given me. I heard the quick intake of her breath.

"More melodrama," I said. "Her name was Jeanie. She got mixed up in a gag that kind of backfired. Learned a little too much. Not as much as you, however."

She let the springy photographic paper roll itself up again. Her fingers were clumsy in replacing the rubber band.

"Did . . . did you—"

"No," I said. "I had nothing to do with it. If that's what you're asking. I would have stopped it if I could. Like I'm trying to stop another one, now."

She said, "What's that other paper?"

"Exhibit Two," I said, and handed it over. She unfolded it, read the official-looking title and the first line, and looked at me quickly, her eyes wide and startled. "But," she whispered, "but this is—"

"A marriage license," I said. "Oh, it's quite genuine. I had to wait twenty-four hours before they would issue it, or I'd have been here yesterday. No blood test is required in this state. All we need is a minister or justice of the peace."

"I . . . I don't understand. Do you really mean—"

"Look," I said, "it's very simple, really. First, there's the legal principle that a wife can't testify against her husband. Just how that applies to things that happened before the marriage, I'm not quite sure. Nevertheless, it makes a good argument for me to use in persuading certain people to leave you alone because you're not going to talk, anyway."

She licked her lips. "You're not thinking of yourself, of course! If I can't testify—"

I said, "Honey, you'd be surprised how little it means to me, personally, whether you testify or not."

"Don't," she said breathlessly, "don't call me honey!"

"I'm sorry," I said. "The second point is a little more complex. It's based on the fact that there's a man who owes me something, and is very conscious of it. He isn't going to take my word for it that you'll keep your mouth shut; nor is he going to leave you alone just because I say so. But if I stake a claim, so to speak; if I can show that you actually belong to me—"

"Do you—" She had to swallow and start over. "Do you

think I'd do *that,* even to save my life? How are you planning to force—"

I said. "Mrs. Wallace, the trouble with you is too much imagination. Ever since we've met, you've been seeing yourself beaten and murdered, and now married against your will to a man who, it seems, makes your skin crawl. And nothing has happened, has it? You're sitting there quite intact with a loaded gun in your lap. I haven't the slightest intention of forcing you to do anything. This is merely a suggestion. I've showed you the alternatives. The picture or the license."

"But you can't be *serious*—"

"I'm very serious," I said. "Of course, I may be wrong. You may not be in as much danger as I think. It's possible that nothing will happen. It's even possible that if it does, the local police and that gun I've given you will suffice to protect you. But I can't protect you unless you give me a little more leverage to work with. If I merely moved in as your bodyguard, he would take it as a challenge, and your sister would have a pitched battle in her barnyard. I've got to demonstrate that I have a personal stake in this; that I'm not just protecting you to be perverse. Do you get it?" She was silent. I don't suppose she understood my grimace, before I went on: "It would, of course, be a marriage in name only, to coin a phrase. Furthermore, I can assure you that there will be ample legal grounds for divorce or annulment when the danger is past."

She said, in a different tone, "You *are* serious, aren't you? I think. . . . I almost think. . . ."

"What?"

"That you're being very nice. Very generous."

I laughed. "I can assure you, Mrs. Wallace, that being married to me is far from a privilege."

She asked, "Why do you care what happens to me?"

I said, "You got mixed up in something through no real fault of yours. I was responsible, to a large extent. I still feel responsible."

"That's hardly a reason for getting married."

I said, "Well, hell, maybe I like your looks."

She laughed abruptly and said, "Maybe that's what I'm afraid of, Mr. Nyquist." After a moment, she said, "You must see that it's utterly ridiculous. You do see that, don't you?"

I said, "This is the place for the line that goes: why, we hardly know each other, Mr. Jones!"

She smiled. "Well, it is a point, isn't it? Anyway, I'm awfully flattered by the proposal, but I'm afraid the answer is no."

I said, "Well, it was worth a try. Have you still got that big rifle of mine? I'll take it off your hands, unless you want to keep it as a hostage."

"No," she said, getting out of the car, "no, frankly, I'll be glad to be rid of it. It's in the trunk of my car, I didn't know where else to put it." She felt the pockets of her jeans. "I think I've g... ... keys. No, they're in the ignition."

"I'll get them," I said. "I see you got that fender straightened." I looked at her for a moment. Well, nothing could have come of it, anyway. I said, "Keep that gun handy, but for Christ's sake keep it where the kids can't get at it. Here's the rest of the shells. You might try a little practice when you get a chance. If you want to buy more, it's the 9-millimeter Luger cartridge. Most sporting-goods stores carry it."

I got the Springfield in its trombone case out of the trunk of the Chevy convertible, threw it in the back of the station wagon, and drove off without looking back.

chapter eighteen

DRIVING BACK toward Capital City I no longer had to worry about being followed, so I cut east to pick up U.S. 147, which has recently been dual-laned clear through the state—an accomplishment to which Governor Maney points with pride, although the project was initiated by the previous administration. It was about noon when I reached the junction. Waiting for an opening, I watched the big trucks roll past and decided I couldn't take that kind of traffic on an empty stomach. There was a filling station on one corner and an eatery on the other. I drove in, parked, went inside, and had a hamburger and milkshake. When I came out, a big car was just swinging out of the southbound lane toward me. There was something familiar about it. I stepped back into the doorway. The big gray Lincoln shot past, heading west, the direction from which I had come. It was Brooks's car and Brooks himself was driving. He had two jerks with him.

I thought about it as long as it took them to get out of sight. At the Lincoln's rate of acceleration, that was hardly more than a second. Then I got behind the wheel, backed the Plymouth out of its slot, skidded it around in the gravel, and sent it after the big car. I cut in the overdrive and bore down on the gas. Some people can shoot straight and some can drive fast. I can shoot. It was twenty miles back to Grantsville and I almost killed myself four times, but I never caught a glimpse of them. The farm was seven miles farther. They were already in the yard when I came over the last rise. I turned the Plymouth into the bushes, grabbed the trombone case, scrambled through the barbed wire, and headed out across the field.

They were leaving now. Two of them had the girl and were leading her to the car. I might as well have saved myself the trouble of teaching her to shoot. The third man had the sister and kids backed up against the kitchen door like a family portrait. I could just barely make it all out at the distance, as I ran diagonally across the field toward a spot from which I could cover the dirt road leading out of the place. The furrows were straight, and deep for running. The young corn was just coming up. Habit had me trying to avoid the plants as I ran, which made it something like a game of hopscotch. I stopped that foolishness.

The third man backed away from the house, turned, and jumped into the car. The Lincoln seesawed back and forth once in the yard, and headed out. There was no time to get any further. I threw myself down, broke the case open, and ripped apart a box of shells. I was breathing like a bellows and my heart was pounding; hardly the conditions for good shooting. There was no time to load the magazine. I threw a shell into the chamber of the Springfield, shoved the gun out ahead of me, and got the picture in the scope, reminding myself that it was still set for Martin Maney at better than four hundred yards, which would make it shoot almost a foot high at a hundred and fifty, the range at which I was prepared to take them as they came down the road.

It was a moving shot, and I led the front tire appreciably, swinging with the car as it rushed toward me. I was dimly aware that I had been spotted; a jerk was popping at me from the rear window with some kind of an undernourished automatic. The little metal-jacketed bullets were hitting short and ricocheting over my head. No matter what has happened to you, you can never quite keep from cringing at the blind, nasty, quavering sound of a ricochet, particularly when you know what kind of a hole one of the crazily spinning slugs will tear if it happens to hit.

I had a mark for the range; a clump of grass along the road. The scope picked it up, my finger obeyed the automatic signal, the gun fired, and the tire went out. I threw the bolt, slapped in another shell, and took the rear tire as, after passing in front of me, they went away. The gas tank was a bigger gamble; there was more than a small chance of the bullet being deflected upward into the body of the car. Well, it was a chance she would have to take. I had a third shell in place, and pressure on the trigger, when the big Lincoln, now bouncing and flapping along on only two good tires, came to a halt. Brooks and the jerks boiled out on the far side, hauling the girl with them.

I drew a long breath of relief. They were pinned in the road in the middle of the field. There was nowhere they could go from there. I opened the gun and loaded up the magazine. Then I got my arm into the sling and drew it up tight. Most people don't know it, but a rifle sling is used as much for steadying the gun when you're shooting as for carrying it when you're not.

Somebody had opened up down there with a heavier weapon, but a hundred yards is extreme range for the biggest pistol made—even in expert hands—and this was closer to two hundred, now. One bullet hit about ten yards off to the right; the rest were short. I swung the scope over there and picked up Brooks; he was crouching behind the hood of the car, sighting carefully with both hands on the revolver and his forearms braced. I held a foot low and rested my finger on the trigger, and Brooks was three ounces from being dead. I had that ugly, God-like feeling of holding a man's life in my hands. I had never liked him.

I saw him shoot again, and heard the bullet sing by overhead. He must have held ten feet high on that one. It was kind of pitiful. He could just as well have been throwing rocks at me, while I could pick him off whenever I chose. I drew a long breath and released the trigger and stood up. He fired again. I don't know where that one went. I threw back my head and let him hear me laugh.

Brooks stood up and put his gun away. After a moment he stepped out from behind the car. The girl was with him. They came across the field toward me, walking side by side. You had to hand it to the guy. He could recognize a losing hand when he saw it. One of the jerks would have tried some kind of a bluff with a gun in her back.

They stopped in front of me. The kid was pale, and there was a reddish bruise on her cheek, and dirt on her jeans and white dickey. She had lost her glasses somewhere. She was always getting messed up around me, it seemed. Brooks was mad.

"You win this one," he said. "For whatever good it does you. But one day we'll meet up when you haven't got that fancy gun along."

I said, "Relax, Brooksie. I just saved you from making a mistake."

"The mistake was yours," he said. "We'll be back."

"No," I said. I held out my left hand. The girl looked at Brooks. He said nothing. She came forward carefully, keeping well out from between us. She stopped beside me. I put my left arm about her bare shoulders and drew her closer, turning her to face him, still keeping the Springfield steady under my right arm. "Go back to the big guy," I said. "Tell him he made a mistake. This is my girl. We're getting married this afternoon."

Brooks looked at me for a moment longer. He would have loved to kill me. Maybe I should have killed him. But Carl would have been unhappy about it; and I didn't want Carl unhappy.

"Congratulations," Brooks said, and turned on his heel and walked off.

chapter nineteen

THE TOWN was named Wilford. The jewelry store was a hole in the wall sandwiched in between a hardware store and a movie theater that had gone out of business and was now, apparently, being used for revival meetings. Since TV, there were lots of theaters like that around. She waited in the car while I made the purchases.

"Here," I said, getting back in. "Put this on." I dropped one of the little packages into her lap, started the car, backed out into the street, and drove slowly ahead. She opened the box and looked at the contents. After a little, she removed her white glove and pulled off the rings she was wearing and dropped them into her purse. When she hesitated, I said, "Put it on, kid. You've got about three minutes to be engaged in. The place is right down the street here, somewhere." After a moment, I said, "We could have saved money by using the rings you already had, but I thought you'd rather keep your memories separate. Here's the place."

It was a white clapboard house behind a white picket fence. There was a neatly lettered sign beside the gate. I looked at the girl. She was very close to tears. I suppose she was remembering the other time. It doubtless seemed very beautiful and romantic in retrospect. There was nothing I could do for her on that score. I pulled up under the tulip poplar that overhung the street, got out, and walked around to open the door for her. Then we stood there a moment pulling ourselves together. I had changed to respectable clothes. She was wearing the striped blue-and-white summer suit in which I had first seen her, with the matching little hat. The outfit had a freshly washed and ironed look. Her blue and white pumps were newly cleaned and her lipstick was straight.

She blew her nose, returned the handkerchief to her purse, and looked up at me. "Let's get it over with."

"Check," I said.

It didn't take long. They waved goodby to us from the door. We drove off in silence. She looked at the two new rings on her finger and pulled her glove back on. I turned right at the first intersection. She looked at me quickly.

"What's the matter?" I asked.

"I thought—"

"What?"

"We came the other way."

"That's right," I said. I was getting a little fed up with the performance. After all, she wasn't the only person in the world with feelings and memories. I didn't give her any help.

She hesitated. "Where are we going?" she asked at last.

"We'll swing west," I said. "Give Brooks time to make his report and Carl time to simmer down. By tomorrow it ought to be safe to go home."

"Home?"

I said, "1434 Western Boulevard. The apartment is right over the shop. It's not a bad place, even though the neighborhood is pretty crummy." She was silent beside me. I pulled off the road and stopped. "What's the matter now?" I asked, facing her. "Did you think you were just going to take a little ride, have a man say a ceremony over you, and go back to your sister's? Just what would that have accomplished? Do you think Carl Gunderman is a fool? Do you want your sister and her kids to have to cope with more men with guns? If Carl thinks we're putting something over on him . . . ! Anyway, it seems to me you'd have sense enough to *want* to get yourself and your troubles away from that farm, before one of those kids stops a bullet meant for you."

She did not say anything. I started the car again. The thunderstorm that had been piling up in the west was getting high enough to block off the sunshine. Presently it cut loose with a few drops of rain, some vicious gusts of wind, and then all the rain in the world. I pulled off the road. We sat it out for about ten minutes. The wind was so strong that the car bounced around on its springs, just parked there. There were leaks here and there around the doors and windows. After a while the storm settled down to a steady drizzle. We started off again. Half an hour later it hit us again with everything in the book. We sat that one out, too. It might have been fun, had there been anyone to talk to. I usually get a big kick out of a thunderstorm. The girl just sat there, drawing in her legs and skirt to avoid the drips and splashes.

"Some honeymoon," I said.

She glanced at me, but did not speak. The worst of it passed over and I started the car again. We drove until eight o'clock through steady rain, the tires hissing and the windshield wipers clacking. We came out on U.S. 401 just north of Larksburg. I had been out this way a couple of times for mountain grouse, and thought I knew a place to stay, but they had the No Vacancy sign lighted when we got there. Heading up the line I found another place, ducked into the office, asked for twin beds, and settled for two doubles at twice the price. They had a restaurant and bar. I got back in the car. The woman who ran the place led the way under a big umbrella. I carried the stuff inside, wrote Mr. and Mrs. Nyquist on the registration card with a steady hand, gave the woman eleven bucks and closed the door behind her.

"Do you want to clean up a little?" I asked the girl, who was still standing by the door. Her thoughts annoyed me. They showed in her eyes. She nodded, and took over the bathroom for a while. I had a drink, waiting. She noticed the bottle the minute she came out. It was more evidence for the prosecution. I said, "Help yourself," and took my turn in the john.

When I came out, she was sitting on the edge of the nearest big bed, waiting for me. I cleared my throat to make a little speech, but changed my mind. It was something else I preferred not to do on an empty stomach.

"Come on," I said. "Let's get something to eat."

Aside from the food, which was good, it wasn't much of a dinner. There was no incentive to linger over the coffee. I paid and followed her out. It was dark outside, and still raining. We ran for the cabin. I unlocked the door and turned on the light, and closed the door behind us, and put my back to it.

"Look, kid," I said.

She swung around to face me. "I'm not a kid," she said.

"All right," I said. "Barbara."

"What is it?"

"The name is Paul," I said.

"What is it, Paul?"

I put my shoulders squarely against the door. It was quite a thing to have to say.

I said, "Look, there's something I want to tell you. . . ." I stopped. It was quite a thing, all right. I said, "Did you ever read an old book by Hemingway? Ernest Hemingway? It's about a nymphomaniac, a Jew, a bullfighter and a character who was damaged in a certain way. Well, I had a hunting accident once." I saw her eyes widen slightly. She did not move. I said, "It walks, it talks, it sleeps, it eats. It's practically human. It's capable of all normal activities, in fact, except one. I hope I make myself clear."

I cleared my throat. "I thought you'd like to know. I wouldn't want any worries disturbing your sleep. As you can see, you're perfectly safe. Furthermore, I have reason to know it's adequate grounds for a divorce in most states including this one. I hope that answers any questions you may have. Don't wait up for me."

I detached myself from the door, turned myself around, located the knob, and got the hell out of there.

chapter twenty

WE DROVE into Capital City at about ten the following morning. It had rained all night, but the sun came out as, coming in by Western Boulevard, we passed the sign of the gun club. I pointed it out to her.

"That's where we test our guns," I said.

"Oh."

Ten minutes later we were home. I pulled into my usual spot in front of the shop. The streets were drying now in the bright sunshine. Everything looked fresh and clean. I had a headache as big as a house. I carried the suitcases into the entrance, left them at the foot of the stairs, and made another trip for the woodchuck rifle and the rest of the gear. The Springfield I had thrown into a marsh forty miles west of town, along with Whitey's P-38. I'd had some notion of wiping the slate clean of evidence, so to speak, but now I regretted the action. If anybody wanted me, they would get me without evidence. Meanwhile two good guns were rusting in the muck. I felt like hell. I also felt like a damn fool. No reason is ever good enough for drinking too much, the next morning.

I stopped her as she started up the stairs. "Come on into the shop and meet the folks."

She paused by the door, a little bewildered by the jumble of lathes and workbenches; the racks and stacks of guns. I guided her forward.

"Don't lean up against anything. It's apt to be greasy. This junior-grade genius is Jim Hines. And that slender character over there is Gustaf Hoffmeyer. Boys, this is Mrs. Nyquist. You can call her Barbara."

There was the kind of scene you'd expect under the circumstances. They were very surprised and very nice. There was hand-shaking and back-slapping and congratulations. As we were going out, Hoffy called to me.

"Oh, I forgot to tell you. Your friend said for you to call when you got in."

"Which friend?"

"How many friends you got, *hein?* This is the big friend with the loud voice." He didn't like Carl Gunderman.

"Okay. Thanks, Hoffy."

She carried the suitcases up the stairs. I followed with the rest of the junk. I had slipped the catch on the upper door when I left. She waited beside me while I unlocked and opened it. We looked at each other, both thinking the same thought, I guess. I put down the stuff I was holding and took the two bags from her and put them down.

"What the hell," I said. "We might as well do this right." I picked her up and carried her inside and set her on her feet again and went back for the luggage. When I had it all inside she was still standing there, looking around the room. Suddenly it didn't seem like much of a room, although I had always been comfortable there. I said, "If that moose makes you uncomfortable, I'll take him down. I always did think the taxidermist gave him a mean look. Of course, he didn't look too pleasant when he was coming at me."

"Did he charge you? I didn't know they were dangerous."

"I didn't know it either, or I'd have stuck to hunting deer," I said. Then I read the question in her eyes, and grinned. In a way, it was a relief to have the confession off my chest. Having her know wasn't quite as bad as I had expected it to be. I said, "No, that's not the gentleman who did the damage. That was a boar, and I didn't keep the trophy.... Well, the kitchen's over here.... The stove and refrigerator work; that's about all I can say for them. Two bedrooms, bath, closet space. Southern exposure, sixty-five a month, and a tin roof that's guaranteed to make the place unbearable after two o'clock every summer afternoon. There's a big fan in the bedroom window that helps a little." She had picked up her suitcase. I pointed out the proper door. "That room over there. It's all yours. If you'll excuse me, I have a telephone call to make."

Carl wasn't at the office, or at home. I finally tracked him down at the Palm Inn, his joint just outside of town.

"What the hell kind of gag do you think you're pulling, boy?" he roared.

I said, "Pipe down, buster. I can hear you."

"What is the big idea of shooting up my boys?"

"If I'd shot them up," I said, "you'd be burying them today. A couple of tires won't break you. What's the big idea of kidnaping my girl?"

"Your girl!" he shouted. "What kind of a screwball deal is that, anyway? What's this about your getting married? Who do you think you're kidding, anyway? This is Carl, boy. Don't give me that stuff."

I said, "It's like they kept telling me at the hospital, Carl. Even if the worst was true, sex isn't everything, they said."

"Yeah," he said. "That's okay for you, but what about the dame? What did the two of you do last night, play pinochle?"

It didn't bother me. I laughed. "You go to hell, Carl. I wouldn't try to explain it to you. There are finer things, you know."

He made a disrespectful sound. "Well, I want to meet this babe," he said. "Come over to the club for dinner. About eight. And if you're not wearing a dinner jacket, I'll have Brooks throw you right out again, see?"

"Brooks," I said, "and who else?"

He laughed. "You bastard. Brooks will kill you one of these days, and I'll die laughing. Eight o'clock. I'll be seeing you."

I put the phone down, and looked up. The girl was standing in the kitchen doorway, although I had not been aware of her coming out of the bedroom. I could tell nothing from her expression. She had removed her hat, the sleeves of her jacket were pushed above her elbows, and she was holding a spatula.

"I put on some coffee," she said. "Do you like your eggs up or over?" We hadn't stopped for breakfast.

"Up," I said.

"How many?"

"Two," I said. "But you don't have to do it. There's a place right around the corner."

"It's all right," she said. "But you'd better come in and show me how to work the toaster. It looks to me as if it's wired for sound." Ten minutes later, when we were sitting down at the kitchen table to eat, she said, "You're not being quite fair, are you?"

"Fair?"

"You haven't given me a single opportunity to apologize."

"There's nothing to apologize for."

"Don't be noble," she said. "I acted like a prissy little fool yesterday. I seem to have a positive genius for jumping at the wrong conclusions."

I said, "It was a perfectly natural jump to make."

She said, "Oh, stop being polite or I'll throw this egg at you!"

I looked at her, startled. Then I grinned. She flushed, and laughed. After that we talked about different things. She was a good kid, and she was trying—we were both trying—but you couldn't say it was a relaxed and comfortable meal. She wouldn't take any help with the dishes, afterward. I went out into the living room and cleaned up the .222 and hung it on the rack. I put the rest of the equipment away, and sat down to read the mail. Presently she came out of the kitchen and paused to brush herself off.

"I'm going to have to get my clothes from the Y," she said. "I can't live indefinitely in just this suit and a pair of jeans."

"Take the car," I said, and got up to give her the keys. "We'll have to figure how to get yours up here. . . . Oh, wait a minute. Have you got an evening dress?"

"Yes."

"Good looking?"

"Well, it's five years old."

I reached for my wallet. She watched me peel four fifties from the sheaf of bills. I had been carrying quite a roll lately, thinking it might come in handy if something should slip. "Here," I said. "We're going out to dinner. You want an outfit to impress Carl Gunderman with what a nice girl you are. Nice, mind you. Not sexy. The kind of girl who could marry half a man and never miss the other half."

I spent the rest of the day in the shop, trying to figure out what was wrong with a 6.5-mm. free rifle we had made for a guy that he had sent back saying it wouldn't shoot. International free rifle competition is just about the most exacting type of target work there is, from a gunsmith's point of view, since it not only covers several different ranges, but also prone, kneeling, and standing positions. The gun is called "free" because there are no limitations on stock design or trigger pull, so that you can have thumbholes through the stock, pronged and hooked butt-plates, palm rests and set triggers, that would be outlawed in ordinary U.S. competition.

Because of the variations in grip and sling tension, it's much harder to make a gun shoot well from several positions than from one. I finally located a point in the fore end that could be made to bear against the barrel by an extreme sideways pull on the sling. He must have been a contortionist for it to cause him trouble, but it was his gun and he was paying the bill. His shooting position was none of my business. I scraped the wood down, reassembled the gun, and beat out a letter of apology on the company portable. Then, just for the hell of it, I loaded up a bunch of 6.5-mm. shells according to the figures under the job number in the testing book. The Plymouth was still out shopping somewhere. I borrowed Hoffy's ancient Pontiac and drove out to the range and checked that musket cold, hot, and in every position including upside down, just in case the guy decided to shoot standing on his head.

When I came back, the station wagon was parked in front. From the way I was glad to see it, you'd have thought I was an honest-to-God bridegroom. Hoffy had some remarks to make about people who drove off with people's cars and didn't get them back in time for dinner. I told him he could afford to miss a meal or two, closed up the shop, and went upstairs. A small ironing board was set up in the living room. The iron, upright, had been left on top to cool. Three dresses and the light suit she had been wearing, freshly pressed, on wire hangers, were suspended from the top of the door of the overcoat closet. She called to me from the bedroom.

"I'll get my junk out of there in a minute. I thought I'd better take a shower before you came. The bathroom's all yours."

"Check."

"I moved some of your stuff into the other room. I hope you don't mind. Your dinner jacket and things are in there. If I missed anything, just yell."

"Roger."

I shaved, showered, and dressed, using a soft shirt instead of the one she had laid out. To hell with Carl Gunderman and his notions of respectability. I also stuck my pipe and pouch into my pocket. I don't know why, but he considered cigarettes presentable, and cigars passable; but a pipe was definitely, in his opinion, unsuited to the pleasantly formal atmosphere he tried to maintain in his club. Well, I had no intention of developing lung cancer just to please him.

The living room had been cleared when I came out. I stood there for a moment, absently reaching for the pipe. Then the bedroom door opened and she came toward me and stopped. The dress was white, of that rather stiff, textured material that is called, I think, piqué. The skirt was wide and did not reach the floor; the bodice was snug, strapless, and had a kind of cuff at the top that kept her from looking, as so many of them do, as if she had accidentally appeared in public in her corset.

"Well?" she said. "It's a little sissy, but I thought that was what you wanted."

I don't suppose she was the most beautiful girl in the world; and the fact that I came close to thinking so, at the moment, was a dangerous symptom. I cleared my throat and said, "It's fine."

"Thanks," she said dryly. "Your enthusiasm gives me courage to go on."

"Really," I said. "You look fine."

"I look like a schoolgirl," she said. "Not like a recently remarried widow of twenty-five. Here. Put these in your pocket. I might want to see something." She handed me her glasses.

"Put them on," I said.

"Look, I have to live with them the rest of the time, but I draw the line at wearing them with an evening dress."

I said, "Honey, they're part of the act. Put them on."

"Well, all right," she said. "If you put it that way." The glasses gave her an earnest, innocent look. She studied me for a moment. "You don't look so bad yourself. Do you mean to tell me there's a man who can tie one of those things himself? Hank always had me—" She broke off, and continued after a moment, "Brief me on this, will you? There must be a couple of things I ought to know."

"Just one," I said. "Don't encourage Carl unless you want him. If he gets the notion that you're available, nothing will stop him short of a bullet, or an axe. I won't go into details, but he'd think it was a great joke on me. That's the way his mind works. He's going to make a try, you can expect that. You'd better know when you go in there what your response is going to be."

She looked at me for a moment longer. "Will you back me if I slap him down?"

"Only if you mean it," I said. "Only if you make it clear from the start that you mean it. Don't think you can kid him along and then have me pull you out of the hole. Carl doesn't kid and I won't pull. Besides, the choice is yours. I wouldn't want to interfere."

She said stiffly, "That wasn't a very nice thing to say."

I said, "Damn it, you don't owe me a thing. I got you into this and I'm trying to get you out. But I can guarantee nothing. If you can do better for yourself elsewhere . . . Ah, hell. Let's go."

"Yes," she said. "Let's."

chapter twenty-one

RAOUL, the headwaiter, saw us coming, and passed some kind of a signal along. The orchestra, which had been playing sweet music for digestive purposes, stopped. The place was about half full. Everybody looked up at the silence. The boys drew a deep breath and hit the wedding march hot and hard. Mendelssohn wouldn't have known his baby. I stopped at the head of the steps and found the kid's hand and wrapped it around my arm.

"There's nothing to it," I said. "All you have to do is walk. A child could do it."

She glanced at me and laughed. "Who's scared? Is that Gunderman?"

"If it's twice as big as life and three times as ugly, it's Gunderman. Did you know you're the prettiest girl in the room?"

"It would sound more convincing if you'd looked around."

"Who needs to look?" I said, and then we were across the damn dance floor. I said, "Hi, people. Babs, that's Carl Gunderman over there. Don't have anything to do with him. And Carla McMahon. Mrs. Nyquist. . . . Carl, you bastard, give us a drink and shut off that damn music and those spotlights. We didn't get married just to entertain your customers."

Carl waved his hand. The musicians went back to Johann Strauss and the lights went elsewhere. Carl stepped forward. "Well, I'll be damned," he said. The kid looked pint-sized in front of him. He was one hell of a big man. He reached down and took her glasses off and laid them on the table. He looked at her again. Then he kissed her. She gave him about ten seconds, and brought her high heel down on his toe. He straightened up sharply, and for an instant his face was ugly. Then he threw his head back and roared with laughter. "Baby, you're okay," he said. "Here, this is for you. A wedding present."

She put her glasses back on, and worked her way through the ribbons and fancy paper to the jeweler's box beneath. Opening this, she gasped. The stones were too big to look real, and there were plenty of them.

"Allow me," Carl said, and clasped the thing about her wrist. "And here's for you, you big lug," he said, producing an envelope which he gave to me. I opened it. It held a certificate entitling me to lifetime service, for any automobile I might own, at the Acme Auto Laundry.

We did not get home until after one o'clock. I switched on the light. Barbara sat down and pulled off her shoes with a little sigh. Then she lay back lazily in the big chair, and watched me shed my coat, tie, and cummerbund. I went into the bedroom and switched on the fan. It was still pretty warm. The fan set up a pleasant draft through the apartment.

"Drink?" I asked.

"I shouldn't," she said, "but I will. Anything you're having." I went out into the kitchen. Presently she called to me, "Who was the snooty blonde? I never did get the name."

"McMahon. Carla McMahon."

"What?"

"Carla McMahon."

"I can't hear you." The fan made quite a bit of noise in the living room.

"I'll be out in a minute," I said. I carried the glasses out, and put one in her hand. "The snooty blonde's name is Carla McMahon," I said.

"Oh. That was a lovely dress she was wearing."

"She can afford it."

"Your friend was giving her a pretty rough time, toward the end."

I said, "He'll get rougher, if he hasn't already." I pulled a straight chair around and sat down. "She's already set some kind of a record, from the looks of things. She's held him off since Monday. Four days. That's about as long as any woman's been able to keep Carl acting remotely like a gentleman."

"You don't sound very sympathetic."

I said, "I'm sympathetic as hell. To him. She's just slumming. Visiting the underworld. But he doesn't know it. He thinks he's got a chance. That's all that keeps him in line, the thought that he's got a chance with a really high-class babe. Society stuff."

"You mean, he'd marry her?"

"Like a shot," I said. "It's his dream. But she's just playing. Wouldn't you say?"

Barbara nodded. "I think you're right."

I said, "Well, it's a little tough on Miss McMahon, I suppose, but she asked for it. I can tell you precisely how it'll go. He'll pop the question, and she'll laugh in his face, and it'll be just too bad. She'll find herself flat on her aristocratic back with her lovely dress up around her neck before she knows what's happening. Well, it isn't as if it hadn't ever happened to her before. That Wendover Hills society crowd isn't noted for chastity." I looked at the kid. She was wriggling her toes thoughtfully inside her stockings. "What's the matter? Do you think I'm being callous? Should I load up a gun and drive out there to protect her? She's undoubtedly fool enough—self-confident enough—to stop by his place for a drink."

I set my glass aside, rose and walked over to the rack and took down the .45 service automatic with the target sights. There have been lots of slurs cast upon that gun, but it's still, in my opinion—except for the fact that you have to cock the hammer by hand for the first shot unless you're fool enough to carry a cocked gun around—the best and most reliable all-around handgun made. The mushhead who talked the services into adopting that damn little pipsqueak carbine instead just didn't know the score. If you can carry a carbine you can carry a real rifle. The pistol's for the poor damn character whose hands and back are already loaded up with something else. Well, that's an old argument, and maybe I'm prejudiced because I happen to be able to shoot a pistol after a fashion. I found a loaded clip in the drawer, and rammed it home.

"Honey," I said, "say the word and I'll go rescue your blonde. Just call me Lancelot Galahad Nyquist, Incorporated. Ladies in distress, our specialty."

She laughed. "I suppose I'll get used to all these guns, sooner or later. Put it away, Paul. I was being silly. But . . . well, to be frank, I found your friend pretty repulsive."

I sat down and picked up my drink. "Carl's pretty much of a sonofabitch," I agreed.

"Then why—"

"Why do I associate with him?"

"Yes."

"It's hard to say. No, it isn't. It's very simple, really. With everybody else I have to put on a front—"

"Why?"

I looked at her quickly; then I laughed. "Honey, there are some afflictions that are serious enough for the guy who's got them, but a big joke to everybody else. Hives, piles, and impotence. . . . Can you imagine what Carl's goons would say if they knew? They'd laugh me out of town."

"But you don't have to associate with Carl and his goons, do you?"

I said, "Back home, everybody knows; hell, it's a matter of public record. I should go back there and make like a tragic figure? Nuts. Here I can be natural with Carl; the jerks I can kick into line; the boys in the shop are good guys and keep their guesses to themselves; and to hell with the rest of the population. . . . As for Carl, well, it's really kind of a relief to have somebody around who knows the story and considers it just a great big dirty joke, as long as there's just one of him. I get sort of tired of being a man with a secret ailment, if you know what I mean."

She hesitated, and said, "You saved his life, didn't you? On that hunting trip. That girl said so. Is that when . . . it happened?"

"Yes." I was surprised to hear that Carl had come so close to talking about it. Miss McMahon must really have got his guard down. After a moment, I added, "Don't think there was any heroism involved. That boar wasn't particular which one of us he got; and I wasn't thinking of Carl when I pulled the trigger."

"His gun had jammed, Carla McMahon said."

"Yes." It was such an old lie, now, that I had no trouble with it at all.

"Then I can see how he might feel . . . a kind of obligation." She glanced at me. "There isn't . . . I mean, there isn't any possibility. . . . Do you mind my asking questions?"

"No."

"Say if you do. I must be pretty tight or I wouldn't pry like this."

"Pry ahead," I said. "How about something to make you tighter? You don't have to keep your head around here, you know. Your virtue is safe with me." I took the glasses, and went out into the kitchen, and returned, put the glass into her hand, and sat down again. "As for the possibilities you were referring to," I said, "it depends upon whether you accept the theoretical testimony of the medical profession, or the practical evidence of my former wife."

She looked up quickly. "Your wife? Oh. That's the girl in the picture in the bedroom? Grace?"

"Yes," I said. I'd forgotten about the picture, and the loving inscription. "Grace."

"She's quite beautiful." There was a noticeable lack of enthusiasm in Barbara's voice.

I laughed. "Grace is all right. Hell, it wasn't her fault. The mistake was all mine; I shouldn't have let her do it. But she came to the hospital, and . . . well, she's quite beautiful, as you say. And the doctors insisted everything was going to be okay; and even if it wasn't, she said, our love would be enough." I shrugged, and drank from my glass. "It wasn't."

"I see." Her voice was careful and noncommittal. I looked at her sitting there, curled up in the big chair. It annoyed me that she should set herself up to judge Grace, as she was clearly doing, on the basis of her own obviously normal and happy, if brief, marriage.

I said, "It was a mess from start to finish. Particularly that start. . . . I don't know who cooked up this propaganda about happy honeymoons; even under ordinary conditions it must be a hell of an ordeal. Ours was a real stinker, as you can imagine; and the situation didn't improve much afterward, either. Liquor got mixed up in it somehow. It was just a completely loused-up operation; and finally she threw some things into a bag one night and stumbled out of the apartment saying she was going to find herself a *man* if she had to pick one up on the street." I did not look at the girl in the chair. "She got her divorce on technical grounds, if you know what I mean. That was fun, too."

Barbara said, "Oh. That's what you meant by its being a matter of public record."

"Uhuh." I looked at my glass, and grinned at her. "This stuff must be potent. I'm really letting my hair down. Now you know the whole sad story. Also, how to get rid of me in a quick and legal way, as soon as this business has simmered down a bit. When the time comes, I'll tell you where to go for your evidence. It's all in the courthouse back home."

"Yes," she said. "Of course." She was silent for a little; then she finished her drink, set the glass aside, picked up her evening sandals, and rose. She looked quite tiny in her stocking feet. Her shoulders were smooth and brown against the white of her dress. I suppressed certain thoughts and emotions; even if I had not promised to behave myself, I'd have been a damn fool to again start something I couldn't finish. I might as well settle for whatever respect this girl might give me. She walked to the bedroom door and turned.

"I don't suppose it's any of my business," she said. "But—" She hesitated, and I saw a little color come into her face.

"But what?"

"Well, it's just that. . . . I mean, what you said about honeymoons. . . . Well, even perfectly normal men, I mean, without any reason for . . . Oh, why don't I mind my own business!" she gasped, quite pink now. "Only lots of other married people have the same. . . . I mean, Hank and I had a simply *awful* time, and it was *weeks* before. . . . It doesn't necessarily mean anything. If you *really* love each other. . . . I sound like a romantic sap, don't I?" She breathed. "You ought to tell me to keep my big mouth shut. Good night."

As she turned away, the doorbell rang.

chapter twenty-two

MARGE SAID, "Be a darling and pay the man, will you, baby? I've lost my purse."

I can't say I was surprised to see her. Being surprised

at Marge was always a waste of time. She was wearing a straight, sleeveless, black tube of a dress, high-heeled sandals, and quite a bit of jewelry. She was carrying a black cartwheel of a hat. Even in the dark doorway I could see that a purse wasn't all she had lost. The taxi driver said he wanted a dollar forty, but he was willing to settle for five. He implied that he had something to keep quiet about. Maybe he had. I closed the door on him.

Marge said breathlessly, "I need a gun, baby. All I want is a gun."

I said, "All you want is five bucks. All you want is a gun. How was Chicago?"

She made a noise indicating her opinion of Chicago. "They'll guess where I was heading. They'll be here any minute, you sap! Give me a gun, goddamn it. I'll kill the—"

"Relax," I said. "Come upstairs and have a drink. I'll take care of the firearms department."

I shoved her ahead of me. When she got to the lighted landing above I could see that the black linen of her dress was dirty and grass-stained down the front; her shoes and stockings were a total loss. The girl certainly was hard on clothes. There was even dirt on her face. It went strangely with the elaborate earrings she was wearing. Barbara was waiting for us in the living room. She had put her high-heeled slippers back on; and she looked neat and lovely by comparison with the taller girl. I could not help comparing her with still another girl I had known, who, much more beautiful at the beginning of the evening, had generally turned pretty wispy and sloppy by this time of night. Well, that was hardly fair to Grace, who had let a noble impulse run away with her.

"Who the hell's that?" Marge asked. "Never mind; skip it. Look, baby, give me a gun and the keys to your car and I'll get the hell out of here before Brooks—"

"First it was five bucks," I said. "Then it was a gun. Now it's the car. Next it'll be a couple hundred bucks for gas and meals and lodging. This could get damned expensive."

"Listen—"

"Sit down and catch your breath, Marge," I said. "Oh. Barbara, this is Marge. Marge, this is Barbara. My wife. Let's have a drink and talk this thing over."

The doorbell jangled. Marge grabbed my arm. I freed myself and walked over to the gun rack and took down the service automatic I had been handling earlier in the evening. I shoved the clip home, jacked a shell into the chamber, set the safety, and tucked the cocked weapon inside my belt, hoping it would not blow my leg off. I never trust a safety very far.

Marge was saying something. I paid no attention to her. I went to Barbara and said, "I don't suppose I can make you stay in the bedroom. Well, if anything happens, flop on the floor and crawl behind some furniture. Never mind your dress or your dignity. Get down and stay down."

Marge said, "If it's Brooks, watch yourself. That bastard would kill you as soon as look at you."

They had discovered that I had left the door unlocked; it had seemed better than going down to meet them in the dark. Carl was first up the stairs. He stopped in the doorway. He had left his white dinner jacket somewhere. His tie was untied and there was lipstick on his shirt and his face was scratched.

I said, "Join the party, Carl."

He stepped inside. Brooks came in after him and took the other side of the doorway. Brooks was neatly dressed in evening clothes and looked, superficially at least, like a gentleman, except that, like Marge, he had taken a spill somewhere in the dark and torn one knee of his trousers. There were no weapons showing except the .45 in my waistband, but it did not take X-rays to locate the gun under Brooks's armpit. His hand seemed to hover in that vicinity. He had seen too many movies. This quick-draw business is the bunk. I've got other things to worry about besides who can discharge a gun faster than whom.

"Is that all the cast?" I asked.

"I've got a couple of boys outside," Carl said.

"You're sure that's enough?" I said. "She's a big girl. She looks pretty tough to me. Maybe you'd better use the phone and call in reinforcements."

Nobody said anything for a little. Marge was rotating the big hat in her hands. She looked down, and seemed surprised to discover that the brim was broken. She threw the hat on a chair. Brooks's hand was still hovering. He wanted it very badly. He wanted it so badly it hurt. He wanted it so badly I could hardly keep from obliging him. If the kid hadn't been there, maybe I would have. There's something nice and romantic—if kind of stupid—about two men facing each other through a blaze of gunfire. It's one way to die. It was a real temptation. But it was not in my line of work. I could have got him, all right, but I did not think I was good enough to keep him from getting off one shot, and there was no telling where it would go, and the kid was standing a couple of feet to my right.

I said, "Carl, call off your dog."

He hesitated, and for a moment I thought we were going to have it; then he grinned. "Okay, Brooksie," he said. "Relax."

I watched Brooks's hand tremble briefly, as if two men were struggling for control of it. Then it dropped limply to his side, worn out from the effort. I looked at the three of them standing there like scarecrows, and laughed.

"God, it must be a rough night out," I said. "What the hell's going on, anyway?"

Carl said, "It's none of your damn business, boy."

"I rent this place. You're here. That makes it my business."

"I warned the bitch," he said. "I told her I wouldn't stand for her mixing into my affairs. I paid her off. I sent her away and paid the fare. I was nice about it. Well, I'm through being nice—"

"Business!" Marge said. "When I stuck my gun in your ear you were damn close to killing her. And you can't kill McMahons in this county, darling. Or even rape them. It's against the law. Smiths and Joneses, okay, but not McMahons. They carry too much weight in the bank."

Carl said, "There was a little misunderstanding, that's all. And maybe I lost my temper a little. But—"

"A little! Hell, she was still shaking like a leaf when we got to her place. Did you know you were a beast and an animal, baby? A vicious animal who shouldn't be let out of a cage?" Carl took a step forward and caught the front of her dress and twisted, pulling her toward him. She showed him her teeth, smiling up at him. "A prehistoric survival, baby, that's you. An uncouth barbarian with delusions of grandeur. A—"

He threw her across the room. She struck the wall and slid to the floor. Barbara gasped and took a step forward. I caught her arm and held her beside me. Marge laughed breathlessly, sitting there.

"Oh, so you're going to do it yourself now! I got away from your bloodhound in the dark. If I hadn't tripped and lost my gun I'd have shot him. So now you're going to take care of the job yourself! But why waste your time with me, baby? Why don't you go apologize to the princess? Explain that you didn't really mean it. It was all a big mistake. It was two other guys who had her down on the couch unwrapping her like a Christmas present—"

Talking, she had pushed herself up, awaiting him. When he reached for her, she sidestepped and struck with her nails across his already scratched face; he caught her wrist, she brought her knee up and he avoided it with the ease of long practice; he slapped her hard across the face with his free hand and pinned her against the wall. She fought him fiercely. They knocked over a chair and an end-table, swept two pictures from the wall, and broke a pottery ashtray I had picked up on a hunting trip out West. It had only cost thirty cents, but I had kind of liked it. I walked over to the corner and picked up a stainless steel cleaning rod in .22 caliber. It was about thirty-six inches long and quite limber. I heard Carl swear and knew that she had bit him. Her dress ripped and she got part of his shirt in return. It was quite a battle, but she was giving away too much weight. He had her cornered and they weren't moving around much any more. Brooks was watching me, looking for an excuse.

I said, "Relax, Brooksie."

I went over to where they were wrestling and lifted the cleaning rod and laid it across his butt with all my strength. It whistled nicely, and cracked like a whip. He jumped a foot, and turned.

"Take it home, Carl," I said. "My wife and I want to get some sleep."

My timing was a little off. He didn't quite see me. For a moment I thought he was going to come at me blind, like a buffalo, then his eyes cleared. He shook his head heavily, and licked his lips. Then he turned and look at Marge.

"Come on, baby," he said.

They walked out together. Brooks looked at me, gave me a chance, gave it up, and went after them. I closed the door and slipped the catch. I lowered the hammer of the automatic and breathed more easily. I crossed the room to pick up the pictures and hang them back on the wall. "Go on to bed," I said. "I'll clean up the mess."

Barbara did not speak at once. I glanced at her. She whispered, "Does that . . . happen often?"

"Every now and then," I said. "I'm kind of the official referee; when it gets close to the shooting or knifing stage they generally bring it here. . . . This was a special occasion; kind of a reconciliation. It was just a matter of getting them face to face and letting them work it out. He was just mad enough to turn Brooks loose on her and Brooks would have got a big charge out of kicking hell out of her and maybe even killing her. Well, you've met Brooks before. I don't have to tell you. Carl would have regretted it afterward, but that wouldn't have done Marge any good." I grimaced. "That guy Brooks is getting to be a problem. I bet he practices drawing that gun in front of a mirror. One of these days I'm going to have to take it away from him; it's guys like that give firearms a bad name." She was watching me without speaking. I said, "What's the matter, kid?"

"You," she said.

"Develop that theme," I said.

"You weren't a bit afraid of him, were you? Brooks, I mean? He was like a snarling animal, and you just laughed in his face. And I bet you stood up to that boar, and that moose, in the same way, didn't you? And maybe you've even got some medals from the war—"

"You've been snooping," I said.

"No. You're just the kind who would have. You're so brave—and such a coward. All the wild animals in the world can't scare you. All the guns in the world don't bother you. But just the thought that somebody might laugh at you behind your back, for something that isn't funny at all and wasn't your fault—"

I said, "Go to bed, kid. Or, if you want to be helpful, get a broom."

Barbara said quietly, "She laughed at you, didn't she? That girl you married. And you couldn't take that. It killed you, for all practical purposes. Being hurt was all right, but being laughed at was unbearable. You made sure it wasn't going to happen again. So you came here—crawling into hiding—and let that dreadful man help you and support you, and in return you . . . you're even willing to commit murder for him. Just so that you can keep your little private hiding place intact!"

I said stiffly, "The shop pays its own way and then some.

So much for Carl supporting me. And as for being laughed at, he kids me about it all the time."

"Yes, *he* does. But he's the only one, isn't he? And you can take it from him because you have something on him, too—"

"Who told you that?" I demanded.

"Nobody told me. Nobody had to tell me. It's obvious, isn't it? Tonight, when you hit him and he turned—like a mad beast!—he would have strangled anybody else, or knocked them across the room with his big fist. He was going to, but then he remembered, and stopped himself. What have you got on Carl Gunderman, Paul? And how long are you going to capitalize on it? Can't you see what it's doing to you, being a parasite to a man like that? And a woman like that! Why, you even get a kind of nasty vicarious satisfaction—"

"Vicarious," I said. "That's a big word, kid, vicarious."

"Well, it's true!" she cried. "You're leaning on him; on both of them. And you don't have to; you don't need them; that's the horrible thing. You just think you do, because a girl laughed at you! You could stand on your own feet—"

I said, "Suppose we continue the analysis in the morning, Barbara. It's getting kind of late."

She looked at me for a moment longer; then she whirled and ran out of the room. The door closed. I went out into the kitchen to get a broom.

chapter twenty-three

IN THE MORNING I heard her in the kitchen when I woke up. Presently I smelled bacon and coffee. She must have stopped by a grocery yesterday, because there had been no bacon in the house. I got up and went into the bathroom. Some of her stuff was in there, neatly arranged beside mine on the glass shelf above the lavatory. It gave me a funny feeling. I was back in the study, clean and shaved, pulling on my slacks, when she knocked on the door.

"Breakfast."

"Be with you in a minute," I said.

She was pouring the coffee when I came into the kitchen. She was wearing blue linen shorts, a striped blue-and-white jersey, and sandals that were mostly thongs. Her hair was pulled back and tied with a narrow blue ribbon. I sat down and made appreciative noises over the food. She sat down facing me. We ate.

"It looks as if we were going to have another hot one," I said presently. "It's warming up already."

"Yes," she said, "it is, isn't it?"

"Did you find the aspirin all right?"

She said, "Yes, Paul, I'm sorry—"

I said, "Skip it, kid."

"It's none of my business," she said. "I should have kept quiet."

I said, "Just remember one thing. Carl and Marge are still human beings, even if you don't like them. And there are times when just any human being can be a big help. . . . I'm going to be needing the car this morning. I hope that's all right with you."

"Of course," she said. "Will you be home for lunch?"

I said, "Sure, if you want to take the trouble."

"It's no trouble," she said. "Don't blow yourself up, or anything."

"I haven't yet," I said, and went out.

Dick Mancuso was going by on his bike as I came out the door. He slammed on his brakes when he saw me.

"Hi, Mr. Nyquist. Hear you got married."

"That's right."

"Guess we won't see you out to the range much any more."

"Oh, I'll be around," I said. "How's that new firing pin holding up?"

"I haven't had a chance to try her yet."

I looked at the newspapers in his basket. It occurred to me that the kid upstairs was probably used to looking at some kind of a morning paper, not being a disillusioned old cynic like me.

I said, "How about putting us on the list, Dick."

"Sure," he said. He pulled out a paper, folded it in the way they have of making it stay together, and handed it to me. "Here you are."

"Won't that leave you short this morning?"

"No, a lady took off on vacation and left me a note."

He rode off, whistling. I tossed the paper up the stairs to the landing, and went into the shop. I had barely got things organized when Jack Williams came in.

I said, "Look, Scoop, I'm busy. And I don't know nothing anyway. All I did was get married."

"Yes," he said, "I heard about that. It's rather an odd coincidence that the girl used to work next door to the office from which Governor Maney was shot."

"Coincidence, hell," I said. "She fingered the job for me."

"I'm not too damn sure that you're kidding." He frowned. "There are too many stray bits of information that don't add up. Like that one. And the fact that Maney visited an oculist the morning he was shot."

I said, "Maybe he wanted to be sure he saw it coming."

"He couldn't see anything coming, with that stuff in his eyes. What do you know about Arnold Brooks?" he asked.

I said, "My God. You mean his name's Arnold? I'll never have any respect for him again." I looked at Williams. "Don't be a damn fool, Jack. If I did know anything, I couldn't tell you."

"Do you happen to know where he was the night Jeanie was killed?"

"No," I said. "Do you?"

"I think so."

"Then, if I were you, I'd keep it to myself," I said.

He said, "If I'm right, I'll get him. I'll get him if it's the last thing I do."

"It probably will be, too," I said.

Out at the gun club, it was hot and bright and calm; a good day except for the heat, which didn't really bother me. Hoffy's stock was fine. Hoffy's stocks are always fine. Patterning the shotgun I had brought along took a lot of walking to tack up the big paper. Shotguns are rated on the basis of the percentage of a given load of shot pellets striking within a thirty-inch circle at forty yards. This was a seventy-percent full choke duck gun that a man wanted opened up to about fifty percent modified because, he admitted, he wasn't a good enough shot to hit anything with the closer pattern. It seemed like a pretty good reason. I ran off five patterns apiece on six different shot sizes. I didn't count them out there. It's a hell of a job counting all those damn little holes, and I thought maybe I could wish it off on Jim Hines.

When I got back to the shop, Jim said, "Your wife was down, Mr. Nyquist. She wants to see you right away."

"Okay," I said. There was no sense asking questions. If he had known more he would have told me, and the answer was just a flight of stairs away. I unloaded the gear in my arms and went up there, and stopped inside the door.

She was standing by the big chair at the end of the room; the chair in which she had sat last night in her white evening dress with her bare feet tucked under her. She was standing in such a way that it was clear that she had just got up, hearing me on the stairs. Whatever it was, she didn't want to discuss it sitting down. She was wearing the crisp light suit in which I had first seen her; the suit in which she had been married. She even had the hat on. The white gloves and purse lay on the little table beside her. She was ready to go. She was holding the front section of the paper in her hand, folded.

"Have you seen this?" she asked.

"I never bother to read the paper," I said. "There hasn't been any good news since Stalin kicked the bucket, and even that hasn't turned out as good as it looked in the first place."

She held the paper out. I walked across the room and took it. Her eyes showed that she had been crying. I opened the paper and read the headline: MANEY ATTACKER CAPTURED, FLOWN HERE. Tony August had managed to get himself into jail in Texas through pulling a knife in a friendly card game. What he was doing playing cards in Texas when he was supposed to be hauling his rump into Mexico at an accelerated rate of speed, the reporter did not say. Various people, including the F.B.I., had been very clever about fingerprints. As a result, Mr. August was now lodged in the Capital City jail awaiting trial on a charge of assault with attempt to kill. There was corroborative evidence, itemized.

I said, "Well, it looks tough for Tony. He might even get his wrist slapped."

"Do you know him?"

"We've met."

"What—" She licked her lips. "What are you going to do, Paul?"

I looked at her, and caught on at last. I was a little

slow that day. It was black and white to her, of course. An innocent man was being persecuted for my crime. As I say, I was a little slow.

I said, "Why, I'm not going to do a damn thing, honey."

"Then—" She licked her lips again. She wasn't going to have much lipstick left, at that rate. "Then I'll have to do it. Unless . . . unless you intend to stop me."

I have never come so close to hitting a woman. I turned away from her and grabbed the .45 automatic off the rack and slapped the clip into it and jacked the shell into the chamber. I didn't even put the safety on. I slapped it into her hand like that, loaded and cocked.

"Pull!" I said. "Just pull the damn trigger! No, point the gun right this way and shoot it. Maybe when I'm dead you'll feel safe at last!"

"Paul, please!"

She laid the gun aside gingerly. I grimaced, feeling foolish, and reached for the weapon and let the hammer down.

"Excuse the melodramatics," I said. "But just what the hell does a man have to do to prove his good intentions around here?"

"I'm sorry."

I unloaded the gun, and put it away, and spoke with my back to her. "Okay. Can we talk about it reasonably now? Or would you rather get a length of clothesline from the kitchen and tie my hands behind my back. Just to make sure I don't absent-mindedly reach out and strangle you."

"I said I was sorry."

I swung around to look at her. "I'm not going down to the police station and offer myself up for Tony August, kid. For one thing, Tony August is a jerk. For another, I wouldn't get within ten blocks of the place if anybody guessed my purpose. For a third, Tony August is being well paid for the role he's playing. And finally, it's very unlikely that anything will happen to him beyond a short term in jail, and he's been there before. If anything else does happen, it's his own damn fault. He wasn't supposed to get caught."

She said stiffly, "They say here the prosecutor is going to ask for the death sentence because you can't reward a would-be murderer just for being a poor shot."

I said, "They'll say a lot of things. It doesn't mean anything. Don't forget there's an election coming up."

She said, "The fact is that a man's in jail for something you did."

I couldn't help grinning. "You're cute as a button, Babs. You learned it all in school, didn't you? Right is right and wrong is wrong."

"Yes," she said.

"The fact is that you don't know what the hell you're talking about."

"Maybe not." She was very close to tears. "But I know what I have to do, Paul. I... I should have done it that very first day. I let you talk me out of it then. I don't know why. I just.... No, I don't know. You just acted so... so natural. It was so hard to believe that you... even after I'd seen.... I knew and yet I tried to... to tell myself.... Oh, damn, I wish I wasn't always crying like a baby!"

I said, "Here's a hanky. I'd offer a shoulder, but I don't suppose it would be proper, under the circumstances."

She gasped, "Sometimes I think I hate you!... Why do you have to make it so hard?"

I looked at her for a moment. If I told her the truth, she would probably not believe it; and whether she did or not, a stick of dynamite would have been safer for her to carry around. As long as she thought she had seen a bona-fide murder attempt, she had a chance, although not a good one. She certainly was a hard little girl to protect. This was twice I had started the job and had to give it up.

I walked over to the phone, and looked up a number in the book. "Here," I said. "If you're going to do it, you might as well do it right. That's the number of the *Courier*. Ask for a reporter named Jack Williams.... He was around this morning; he ought to be somewhere where you can reach him. Make him promise to use the influence of his paper to protect you. He's an honest lad and he's been trying to get something on me for a long time. You can probably handle him better if you don't act too fond of me. Your best line would be that of a poor little disillusioned bride without too many brains. You got roped into something accidentally and you're trying to get out. Which is the truth."

I looked at the guns on the rack. There didn't seem much point in weighting myself down. I wasn't going very far. Well, I hadn't been going very far for a long time. It looked as if I was about to get there.

I said, "So long, kid. As we hardened criminals say, I'm taking it on the lam. See you in jail."

chapter twenty-four

I GOT as far west as Gardner Forks, a matter of a hundred and seventy miles. They must have had two cars on my tail, this time, because I had lost one and was celebrating by having dinner when they walked into the place. I kind of regretted not having brought along some kind of a firearm when I saw them. I had been thinking in terms of cops, I suppose. Crooked cops, perhaps, but still cops, doing a job of work. But he had apparently decided to handle it privately. The jerks stopped at the table. There were three of them. I laid down two dollars to cover the meal and forty cents for the waitress; and got up and went out with them. Well, it's like I said once before, the only thing you can do with a gun is shoot it, and even if I'd had one along I wouldn't have fired it in a crowded restaurant.

We went back a lot faster than I had come out. The jerk at the wheel was born crazy, and two hundred horsepower aggravated the complaint. It was still not much past ten o'clock when we pulled into a kind of garage down on Benson Street, on the south side. There were a lot of trucks in the place. I never did learn what the business was. The second floor was a warehouse, with a lot of crates stacked to the ceiling. Back in a corner was a kind of office. Brooks was there.

"Did you have any trouble?" he asked.

One of the jerks said, "It was a breeze. He's a lamb, just a little woolly lamb. Right, bud?" He hit me alongside the head.

"Don't do that," Brooks said. "He's a friend of the big guy, remember. Treat him gentle." He hit me in the stomach. There wasn't any sense in fighting back. It was going to be a long rough evening. I might just as well decide to relax and take it as it came. "Where's the girl?" Brooks asked.

It was obvious that they already knew. "She went to the police," I said.

"Why didn't you stop her?" I didn't answer that one, and he asked, "What made her decide to spill it?"

"An innocent man was in jail for a crime he hadn't committed."

"Tony innocent? Don't make me laugh."

"That's what she said."

"Why didn't you stop her?"

"She's a good kid," I said. "I like her."

"How much does she know?"

"Very little."

"You told the big guy she was in with you; she was standing by for you Saturday."

"I lied," I said. "She walked in on Whitey and me right after the shot. I'd never seen her before. Whitey was going to kill her so I shot him. I held a gun on her and made her take me to her car and drive me out of town. Then I threw a scare into her to make her keep her mouth shut. I'd saved her life from Whitey, so she bought it. Later I went down to sew it up by letting her see what a nice guy I was. I had a marriage license along; but she balked at that, until you boys helped me out by trying to carry her off. She's a good kid and she doesn't know anything except who fired the gun that shot Maney. She still thinks it was an honest-to-God attempt at murder."

"And she's your wife, so she can't testify against you," Brooks said. "All she can do is blow the whole deal skyhigh for everybody else. It's a neat trick, but what makes you think you'll ever see a courtroom? How much did the *Courier* pay you for selling out?"

I said, "Hell, that paper can't even pay their reporters enough to live on."

The jerks moved in on me, and we went over it with variations, for about an hour. If there's any man around who can take a beating in a dignified manner, I'd like a demonstration. Personally, I found it a degrading business. After a while, I got hold of an idea that saw me through. I made a note of the faces of the three jerks. Brooks's face I already knew. I wouldn't forget Brooks. I promised myself that some day, somehow, I was going to kill all four of them. It helped a lot. Carl came in about eleven fifteen and stopped it.

"What the hell's going on here?" he demanded loudly. "I told you to find him. I didn't tell you to kill him." He marched into the middle of the office, knocked the jerks aside, and helped me up, and set me in a chair. "Brooks, you stupid bastard . . . !"

He went on like this for a while. It was a good act. He was wearing light slacks and a gaudy sports shirt with the tails hanging out. The costume seemed to emphasize the fact that he'd been living well for some time now. He was getting to be a hell of a big man in all directions.

I grinned at him. "Save it, Carl. You don't have to impress me."

"You sonofabitch," he said. "I might have known that dame of yours was going to foul things up. Why the hell did you want to go and get mixed up with a dame when you knew damn well you couldn't keep her happy?"

His theory of the incident was obvious and simple and forthright. He thought that Barbara had left me for the same reason Grace had left me, and in the same vengeful frame of mind.

I said, "You've got it all wrong, Carl. The kid's got a conscience, that's all. Even though she loves me dearly, she couldn't stand by and let an innocent man be punished for what I had done. And she still thinks it was meant to be murder; I never told her otherwise."

"What she thinks doesn't make much difference now."

I said, "Sure it does. It just means we trade me for Tony, that's all. The setup remains the same; just the leading character is different."

"Yeah," he said. "Different. Tony didn't know enough to talk in court. You do. And for all I know, the girl does, too. And one peep out of either of you brings down Maney with a crash that'll rock the whole state; figure how it'll look in the papers, that he arranged to have himself shot at! And I can't afford to lose Maney, boy. I've got a lot of plans for Martin Maney—and Carl Gunderman, too."

I said, "The kid doesn't know. I give you my word."

He looked at me for a moment. Then he said, "Okay. But that still leaves you."

"Uhuh," I said. A small germ of an idea stirred in my mind as I faced him. Psychology is a funny thing; I didn't really give a damn what happened next. The kid was gone, as far as I was concerned; and it had only been a kind of wishful daydream anyway. She was safe with Jack Williams; the *Courier* would look after her. As for me, I didn't care. Yet some kind of pride kept my mind working:

here was this big guy in front of me, and I knew more
about him than anybody else in the world; and I ought to
be able to give him at least a run for his money. I said,
with a sigh of resignation, "Okay, Carl. I get your point.
But while you're figuring how to dispose of the body, how
about letting me wash up a bit. Not that it makes much
difference how I look, I suppose; but I'd feel better."

He hesitated, and then laughed. "Boy, you're slipping. If
you think I'm letting you back there alone, to climb out
the window.... Okay, Bert," he said. "Let him wash up,
but keep an eye on him."

I went in the little room behind the office with the jerk
called Bert, filing the name away for future reference. A
careful inventory showed that, aside from a little blood and
dignity, and a chipped tooth, I had everything I had brought
into the place. My face didn't look too bad. It would look
worse later. I went back out into the office, followed by
Bert. Carl put a drink into my hand.

"Have a shot of truth serum," he said. I drank. He said,
as if he had not said substantially the same thing before,
"I knew that dame was going to make trouble."

"They always do," I said. "As the man says, you can't
do with them and you can't do without them."

"*You* can," he said. He never let me forget it for long.
It was the advantage he had over me; and he liked to use
it. I had an advantage over him, too; but I could see no
way of using it here. There was no point in just needling
him to make him angry. After a silence, Carl said, "I'm
sorry as hell, Paul," and in a way I believe he really was.
We had been together for quite a while; we might not like
each other much but we were used to each other. I got
his meaning clearly. What he was saying was that he would
miss me when I was gone. It wasn't really a big surprise.

"Sure," I said.

"I mean it," he said.

"I know."

"Maney wants you. I've got to make the deal. He's on
his way now."

"Sure."

"I can't afford to let him stay mad," Carl said frankly.
"It's already cost me too much money. Besides, I need the
little bastard, and he's no good to me as long as he thinks
he smells a double cross. After the girl's telling him that

you did the shooting and not Tony ... well, you can see how it looks to Maney, like the two of us had tried to pull a fast one on him and then cover up, using Tony as a fall guy. Anyway, he's funny about his health, you know; and even if I could guarantee you'd keep your mouth shut, he wouldn't agree to letting you go free after putting him in the hospital. It's personal with him. He won't settle for Tony; it's got to be you. Any way you look at it, boy, it's got to be you. As for the girl—"

"What about her?"

"He's working on it now," Carl said. "What happens to her depends, I guess, on how many people she got to talk to downtown before he got wind of it, and whether he can shut them all up—"

"He can't," I said. "I sent her to Jack Williams at the *Courier*. Even Maney can't shut up a whole newspaper."

Carl glanced at his watch. "Well, the little blowhard ought to be here pretty soon. Anything I can do for you, boy? Within reason? Another drink, a smoke, a plate of fried chicken? Name it and you can have it."

I started to speak, and checked myself, and said, "No, I guess not."

"Ah, spit it out," he said. He really wanted the opportunity to do something for me, now.

"Well," I said, "if you could get me a clean shirt. . . . It's silly, but I hate to face that little bastard Maney looking like a bad accident."

He could understand that; he had always been a great one for appearances. He swung toward Bert. "Get the boy a shirt and a pair of pants," he said. It was a big deal, pants and everything. "Goddamn it, how do I know where?" he snapped. "Don't tell me it's the middle of the night; I've got a watch. Ah, hell. Where's his keys?" Somebody produced the keys that had been in the Plymouth. He threw them at Bert. "Here. Do I have to tell you the address, too? And don't take all night; Maney'll be here in fifteen minutes. . . ."

I watched Bert leave. Now if I had a little luck, and Hoffy was working late and wasn't too damn absorbed in what he was doing and drew some conclusions from one of Gunderman's jerks poking around my apartment and overcame his natural inertia enough to call the *Courier* or Lieutenant Fleet. . . . I didn't need a little luck; I needed a whole bushel of horseshoes. Well, it was the best I could do; and it didn't make a hell of a lot of difference anyway. Like they say, why take life so seriously; you'll never get out of it alive, anyway.

chapter twenty-five

MANEY WAS preceded by two men who wore the wide hats and khaki summer uniforms of the State Police, which didn't necessarily mean that they were policemen. He had his own private squad—some people said half a dozen, others said a hundred. Since they were carried on various different payrolls and appeared both in and out of uniform it was a little hard to make an accurate tally. They were selected, I had been told, on a somewhat different basis of merit from the state force. They were the reason why I had insisted on doing my shooting from four hundred yards. Their primary duty was, of course, to guard the body, but they had been known to branch out a little now and then. These two inspected the premises, and took up stations by the door. Maney came in, accompanied by two more and an unidentified civilian.

He marched into the room, and came to a halt. It was quite an entrance, for no bigger audience than he had. I suppose he had to keep in practice. The civilian spotted a chair and hauled it around. Maney sat down, reluctantly. Like most short men, he would clearly have preferred to maintain what height he had by staying on his feet; but apparently he was still under doctors' orders.

He was a square little man with distinguished features and dark hair beautifully edged with gray. He was wearing a gray suit of some kind of summer worsted. The arm, in its right-angled cast, was supported by a gray silk scarf. Even in that dingy office, all he needed was a bottle of Lord Calvert. It was hard to realize that this was the same wildman who could turn a political gathering into something resembling a revival meeting—I guess his smooth and polished air made the violence more effective when he turned it on, giving the impression that he was being carried away in spite of himself. He was quite an actor, in one way or another. I had never seen him at close range before.

"Is this the man?" he asked, looking at me.

Carl said, "Yes."

"Why are his hands free?"

One of the tame cops stepped up and put handcuffs on me. I found it an unpleasant sensation.

Maney said, "Bring in the girl. I want to see her make the identification."

I had lived through a good many sickening moments, of various kinds—more than the average man, I guess—but this one was a little jewel, perhaps because of its unexpectedness. There was no reason for her being here; no reason at all. Besides, Jack Williams was supposed to be looking after her.

I said harshly, "That won't be necessary. I'm not denying anything."

Maney said. "We'll hear from you later. We got a confession from that hoodlum we had in jail, too. This time I'm making sure our big friend isn't putting anything over. . . . Bring her in!"

They brought her in. She looked quite small between the two uniformed troopers—small and tired and rumpled, which made it worse. She was still wearing the light, striped suit, and it had been twelve hours, and she had undoubtedly been passed from office to office and hand to hand all day. She had that soiled and wilted look that people always seem to get from waiting around public buildings, particularly on a hot day. Her shoes were scuffed and her gloves were smudged and there was a stain on her skirt—coffee or Coke from some pickup meal she had been given while waiting.

I had done this to her, I told myself; I had brought her here like this. My careless favor to Carl Gunderman—just a couple of harmless shots; and what difference did it make, anyway?—had brought this about. It was no justification to say that I had not meant to hit anybody, to hurt anybody, and that Martin Maney probably deserved to be shot, anyway. Other people had become involved. The girl Jeanie had died. . . . I tried to dismiss that particular thought from my mind, but it would not go.

Barbara stopped inside the door. Maney looked at her and said, "Is that the man?"

She glanced around quickly, and saw me. Her eyes widened

slightly. I guess I didn't look very good, either, despite the fresh clothes Bert had brought me.

She licked her lips. "Yes, it is."

"This is the man you first saw in a room on the third floor of the Wadsworth Building?" He had been state prosecutor before he made the governorship, and it showed. "He was holding a rifle? A shot had just been fired? You had opened the door to investigate?"

"Yes."

"You're sure you had never seen him before that moment?"

"Yes."

"You were employed by the North Star Insurance Company?"

"Yes."

"This company occupies the office next to that from which the shot was fired?"

"Yes."

"We have evidence to prove that this man had been in and out of the building several times during the preceding week. But you never saw him until three o'clock on Saturday?"

"No."

"You're sure of that?"

"Yes."

Maney sighed, for the benefit of the non-existent jury, signaling his giving up of this unprofitable line of questioning. "Very well. Now, there was another man in the room, is that right?"

"Yes."

"And this man—the man who is standing over there—shot down the other man before your eyes."

"Yes. He was going to kill me. The other man."

"And this man, Nyquist, came to your rescue?"

"Yes."

"Very commendable of him, I'm sure. But afterward he held a gun on you and forced you to lead him to your car, which you then drove away according to his instructions. . . ." We worked our way through it in this manner. Every so often he would stop his recital to let her make her response. When he had progressed as far as Wednesday, he paused dramatically, and said, "Mrs. Wallace—I mean, Mrs. Nyquist—do you honestly expect us to believe this story? That on Wednesday afternoon, you, a respectable young

woman, agreed to marry this man whom you had met only
once before, on the previous Saturday, when you had caught
him in the very act of attempting the most dreadful crime
of which a human being is capable, that of taking the life
of his fellow man? How did he explain himself to you?
He must have had some justification, some excuse, some
reason that touched your heart! How else could you bring
yourself to get into his car and drive off with him to be
married—a man who had killed once before your very eyes
and who, except for accident or lack of skill would have
had another life on his conscience: a double murderer, in
everything except accomplishment!"

She was silent.

"Come, young lady," Maney said sharply. "What story did
he tell you? How did he present his case? It must have
been a convincing presentation. It convinced you. You were
willing to bind yourself to him for life, even knowing that
he tried to commit a coldblooded murder. Did he claim
political justification for his act? Had he been led astray
by the rabble-rousing tactics of the opposition and certain
irresponsible sections of the press? Did you consider him,
perhaps, an honest but misguided and impulsive individual
who had been encouraged by false inflammatory propaganda
to feel that the dreadful step he was taking was the right—"

She laughed. It slipped out of her; apparently that
description of me seemed pretty wide of the mark. The sound
of her own laughter startled her. She looked around
desperately, and saw everyone waiting for her to speak.

"He said—" She licked her lips. "He said he was just
doing a favor for a friend."

There was a little silence. She became quite pale as she
realized what she had said. Maney looked at me, and at
Carl.

"A favor, eh?" he said. "For a friend?" After a moment,
he said slowly, without looking at her, "Thank you, Mrs.
Nyquist. Now we know where we stand."

It was very quiet in the place. Whatever business was
carried on around there, they did not transact it at midnight.
Maney got deliberately to his feet. He came forward, across
the room, and slapped me twice across the face, left-handed,
making a clumsy job of it. I heard the kid gasp. One of the
imitation cops silenced her.

"My arm!" Maney said. "It's going to be shorter than

the other! They even ... they even think it might be a little stiff. You've made me a cripple! A cripple!"

He was taking it big. I couldn't seem to feel a great deal of sympathy for him, although it was certainly a serious thing, being a cripple like that.

"A favor!" Maney said. "For a friend!" He stared at me hard. "A friend who has turned on you now. I think it's time we heard from you. Everything."

I said, "Sure, but do we have to have that bitch in here? She's said her piece."

"Governor," the civilian said, "Governor, hadn't you better sit down?"

Maney looked annoyed, but turned and walked back to his chair. He was a little shaky on his pins.

I said, "I'll talk. Just get the double-crossing little tramp out of here before I strangle her with my bare hands. She and her goddamned conscience! After I saved her life twice! I should have let Whitey shoot her. I should have let Brooks have her—"

"All right!" Maney said. "That's enough!" He considered the matter. Then he looked at the man standing by the kid, and jerked his head toward the door. I didn't watch them go out. Maney looked at me. "All right. I want to hear about this favor. I want to hear all about this favor."

I said, "Carl wanted some shooting done. I did it."

"Where did this other man come in? August?"

"The deal looked a little screwy," I said. "Carl decided I needed protection. A fall guy, who wouldn't mind taking a trip. August."

"What was screwy about the deal?" Maney asked. "In what respect was it screwy?"

I said, "Well, I've been asked to shoot at men before. By Uncle Sam. But this is the first time I was ever asked to shoot at a man and not hit him."

I heard Carl give a sigh of relief. I could have fouled him up badly on that one. Just a little lie would have messed up the deal. Maney would have believed it. He was still looking for a double cross. It was a temptation to pull the rug out from under Carl, particularly after the way Brooks and the jerks had worked me over.

But I needed Carl. I needed him to take care of the kid. I looked at him directly, and shifted my glance to the door.

He looked that way, and back to me, and hesitated; then he nodded minutely. It was a deal.

"You're telling the truth?" Maney said. "Your instructions were to shoot and *not* hit?"

I said, "That's right, Governor. Carl played it straight. You've got no quarrel with him."

"But you took advantage of the opportunity—"

I said, "No."

He was out of his chair again. "Then what about my arm? Are you trying to claim it was an accident? Or are you simply such a bad shot—"

He was certainly upset about that arm. I said, "There's nothing wrong with my shooting, Governor. But next time you act as a target it would be a good idea if you'd stand reasonably still."

chapter twenty-six

THEY WERE still at it three quarters of an hour later. Every time it seemed they would finish flexing their muscles, so to speak, and get down to terms, they'd go off again.

"He's your man," Maney said. "Everybody knows he's your man. He could cause me a little temporary embarrassment, to be sure, if he were to tell that story in court, but nobody'd believe—"

"Temporary!" Carl said. "Hell, if it even got whispered around that you'd arranged to have yourself shot at, good-by Senator. Good-by Governor. Good-by Maney." He spat on the floor. "Don't talk courtroom to me. You know damn well you can't let him get inside a courtroom; besides, what's to put him there? The girl can't testify against him. She's his wife. Stop throwing your weight around and talk deal."

"Well," Maney said, "to avoid unfavorable publicity, I might be willing to make a few minor concessions, *if* I were assured of whole-hearted support in the coming election."

Carl laughed. Standing up, in his gaudy sports shirt, he dwarfed the room and the conservatively dressed older man seated before him. There was an air of triumph about him;

the air of a man who had drawn good cards, bet them well, and was now ready to show his hand.

"Concessions is fine," he said. "Concessions is swell. Minor isn't so hot, Governor. You need me. I don't need you. I can break you like a stick and take my chances with the next guy. Politicians I've got coming out of my ears, Governor, even slick politicians like you." He lifted his hand, cutting off interruption, and went on. "You need me. Don't try to kid me. You've got a tough fight this fall and you know it, or you wouldn't have tried to pull this damn fool publicity stunt. People are catching onto you. And why do you think I helped you on this? Because now I've got you sewed up. I've been waiting for you to slip for a long time, Maney. I've been playing along with you, co-operating like a good boy, acting scared of your tame prosecutors, taking orders, paying off, waiting. When you told me—ordered me—to set up this little gag for you, I knew I had you. Well, the bullet went a little too close, for one reason or another, and I had to wait some more, until you simmered down. But that uses up all the waiting I've got on hand, Maney. Do you deal with me or do I get myself another boy?"

Maney said, "If you think—"

"Look," Carl said patiently, "look, Governor, you're on a spot. A bad spot. Stop making faces at me. You need a fall guy who doesn't know anything; somebody to get up in court and take the rap for the shooting, so we can file it and forget it. Tony August. I put him there for you to use; use him."

"They let him go six hours ago."

"Catch him again. Then you need silence. You need silence in big hunks and little ones. Lots and lots of silence. From me. From my boys. From Nyquist, here. . . . I've got a big stock of silence, Governor. It's for sale. What am I bid? What am I offered? What about Jarvis down in the third district? I need him. I asked for him two years ago and didn't get him. I'm asking again. What about—"

Maney blew up and told him how wrong he was. He, Maney, could smash Gunderman and his whole organization simply by picking up the telephone. Just a word to the State's Attorney would do it. . . . They pushed it back and forth for another half hour. Then they kicked us all out and got down to terms.

When I came outside, the kid was sitting out in the

warehouse on a dusty crate, unmarked except for a stenciled: *This Side Up*. Her hands and her purse were in her lap. She looked as if she were waiting in the principal's office after throwing spitballs at teacher. Then she looked at me and the illusion vanished. The light was poor—there were just two lighted bulbs for the whole area and neither was near us—but I could see quite clearly that she was not a kid. Well, neither was I, for that matter; although sometimes you could hardly tell by looking. This Sir Galahad routine, for instance, had been a pretty childish subterfuge, when you came to think of it. I knew now that I had not married her to protect her any more than a man marries any woman to protect her, if she'll let him. I had married her for the good, sound, old-fashioned reasons—but I had not, after one failure, had the courage to admit it either to myself or to her. . . .

She looked at me steadily, asking with her eyes, showing no resentment for what I had called her in the office. She was a bright girl; she had already guessed that I had got her out of there because there were things she was safer not hearing.

I had no answers to give her. The answers were still being made behind the closed door. There was nothing between us that could be spoken here.

I said, "I thought I told you to stick with Jack Williams."

She said, "I did, Paul. They forced his car to the curb when he was bringing me back to his newspaper to write up the story. They brought me here. I don't know what they did with him."

That made it worse, if possible. One of the jerks behind me gave me a push. I moved away obediently, and sat down some distance away from her. It was better that we didn't talk any more. I told the man beside me that I was going to light my pipe, so that he wouldn't get trigger happy. It was quite a trick, with the handcuffs. It kept me busy for a while. Then I smoked and listened to the murmur of voices through the closed door. You could tell Carl from Maney, but you could not hear what either of them was saying.

Presently the door opened and Maney came out. He did not look our way, but walked off with one guard and the civilian in tow. The other guard came over to where I was sitting and reclaimed his handcuffs. They cost seven-fifty a pair, he said, and he wasn't going to leave them behind. He went off after Maney, who was waiting for him impatiently. They took the big service elevator down instead of using the stairs.

Carl came out of the room. He looked at me and looked away. Well, that was expected. The Governor was an eye-for-an-eye man; somebody had to pay for that misplaced bullet. I waited. Carl glanced at Barbara, and turned on his heel, and walked away.

I watched him go. Good-by, Carl. Friendship wasn't enough, it seemed; besides, we had never really been friends, had we? I did not look at the kid, not wanting her to see the sickness in my eyes. Besides, there was no need. She was a bright girl; she would know. Carl was getting what he wanted; what he had always wanted. Maybe there was even a classy blonde involved. After all, Maney was a socially prominent figure and he, Carl Gunderman, was going to be a power in the state. The power in the state; while Maney shifted his operations to Washington, D.C. In return, Carl was taking care of the messy details, like mopping the floors and scraping the chewing gum off the seats. He had sold a chunk of silence; and he was making delivery.

Brooks came into sight from the direction of the elevator; and the jerk beside me rapped me on the shoulder with a gunbarrel as I started to rise. *Not Brooks, Carl!* I thought. *You didn't have to turn her over to Brooks!* I remembered a body on a white table, and a glossy photograph that was still in the glove compartment of my car; and suddenly I knew that I hated Carl Gunderman. Well, I guess it was about time.

chapter twenty-seven

SOMEBODY HAD driven my Plymouth station wagon back from Gardner Forks; it was awaiting us by the stairs. There was a delay while they figured out how to get the rear seat up; I usually keep it folded into the floor. Then I got in there between two of them; and the third got up front behind the wheel, and we took off like a fire-engine answering an alarm. The first block was long enough to allow him to reach fifty-five in second. As we took the corner, the left front tire let go with a bang.

We slewed across the street and back again. There was no traffic at that hour of the night. We had the whole street to play in. We pulled up at the curb. The driver got out to look. I recognized him; he was one of those on the list I had made up in that office. The one on my left hit me across the ear for not having better tires on my car. The third one suggested going back for another car.

The driver said, "Hell, we've got to get this heap to his place, anyway. It's got to look natural. Just an industrial accident, Carl said. Guy that works with guns all day gets his head blown off with one in his shop. Can't have any questions about why his car wasn't home when he was. See if the bastard's got a spare."

"Drive it on the rim."

"I said, it's got to look natural. Does a guy leave his car sitting around on a flat?"

"Well, let him change his own damn tire. Damned if I'm going to mess with it."

They pushed me out. I opened up the tailgate, and shoved gear around until I could get at the spare tire well. Unfortunately I carry no guns in the car normally. It's just asking to have them stolen. I've lost a couple of sets of tools, as it is. I got out the bumper jack and took the weight off the wheel and got it off. The tire had blown wide open. I tried not to look at the hole, nevertheless; and when I rolled the wheel back, I kept it shielded by my body as much as possible. I had just heaved it into the rear of the station wagon when the rifle in the alley spoke again, with the nasty small crack of a .22. The bullet splattered against the building behind us, high up.

A boy's high voice cried, "All right, now! Put your hands up, all three of you ... *Don't!*" The last was a choked little gasp, and the rifle cracked sharply, and a man cried out and dropped a gun and grabbed for his shoulder. "It could have been your eye just as easy." The voice was shaky. "Ask Mr. Nyquist."

I could see him now. I had hoped for Hoffy—prayed for Hoffy—but what I'd got was Dick Mancuso, and I'd settle for that. The boy was lying flat on his belly in the alley, in the shadow of the building. I could see the gleam of the thirty-dollar target rifle. He was using his sling for steadiness, the way he had been taught. Nobody had taught him to shoot at moving targets, like automobile tires, but kids pick up that kind of knowledge on their own time.

I said, "He can shoot you to pieces at this range. He's a crack shot with that gun. And don't think a .22 won't kill you."

Nobody said anything. They didn't have their hands up, but they didn't move, except the man with the wounded shoulder, who leaned back against the car for support. I was glad to see he was the one I would have picked to shoot, given a choice. I walked around the car and came up on the right and got the fallen gun. It was a cinch after that.

Driving away, I said, "Goddamn it to hell, Dick, what are you doing here?"

He said, "Stop the car, will you, Mr. Nyquist? I'm going to be sick." I stopped the car. He opened the door and was. "Do you think I killed him?"

"Hell, no," I said. "Not a chance." I started the car again.

He wiped his mouth on a dirty handkerchief. "Well, it was like this," he said. "I . . . well, I was monkeying around with the gun at home and, well, I took the bolt apart, the way you did the other day, just to see how it worked. Well, I had it all spread out on the dining table and the brat got into it. She gets into everything. She's only two, but she's a menace. I found everything except one little pin and I couldn't find that so I dropped around the shop around six o'clock and Mr. Hoffmeyer fixed it for me and when I was leaving I saw one of Gunderman's creeps sneaking into your place. I went back and told Mr. Hoffmeyer but he was busy carving on a stock again and just grunted, the way he does. So I kind of waited around outside until the goon came back out again carrying some of your clothes. I didn't dig that, so I got on my bike and chased him. He drove pretty fast and I lost him after a while, but I kind of rode up and down and then I saw this garage place and there was your car standing inside. So I waited. When you came out . . . well, the way they were pushing you around, it looked like they was taking you for a ride, so I thought I'd better stop them."

"You'll never have a better thought," I said. "Thanks, Dick."

The apartment was dark when we pulled up in front; so was the shop, except for the usual night light. Hoffy had gone home. I figured I had a little time; they wouldn't expect me to come here. I kept recalling the photograph in my car. The girl in the picture had been picked up before eleven that night, but she had not died, according to the medical testimony, until around three in the morning. Brooks was a slow and thorough workman, who liked his work. . . . I had a little time, but I couldn't afford to use any more of it than necessary. What seemed like minutes to me, here, safe and free, could be hours or centuries to the kid, wherever she was. Dick followed me inside.

I said, "Get me a hacksaw, Dick." I was groping around in a stack of guns. There was an old Model 97 we had taken in trade. For the work I had in mind, that outside hammer was better than a safety. I never trust a safety much. I found the gun and laid it on the bench and took the saw from the boy. "Now find me a box of shells. Twelve gauge. Number 0 or Number 1 Buck. There ought to be some over there."

It was a long-barreled old bastard. I sawed it off a little ahead of the magazine. Rifles are fine in open country. Pistols are strictly emergency rations as far as firearms are concerned. There's nothing you can do with a pistol that you can't do better with some other gun, except carry it in your pants. For dirty work at close range there's only one weapon, if you don't mind being called unsportsmanlike. I didn't mind.

Dick said, "I can't find anything bigger than Number 4 Buck, Mr. Nyquist."

I said, "That's heavy enough. It's not like I was going after something with a lot of vitality, like bear or deer."

chapter twenty-eight

I SAID "Plaza 3-3039. If anybody answers, sound scared and ask if Mom is there."

The boy dialed the number. It was hot with the two of us in the drug store phone booth. I had not thought it advisable to hang around the shop any longer, even to save a dime. I counted ten rings and shook my head. Dick hung up the phone. We got out of the hot booth, walked through the cold store, and out into the warm night.

I said, "Okay, now I'm dropping you off at the streetcar line, Dick. Hightail it to the *Courier* office and tell them to check if they've mislaid a reporter named Williams. Any questions they ask that you know the answer, tell them." I slapped him on the shoulder. "I'll thank you right next time I see you. So long, pardner."

He punched me in the arm. "Don't take any wooden nickels, pal."

I was a big disappointment to him. I was going into action with a sawed-off shotgun instead of two Colts slung low at my hips. I could see him in the mirror some time after I pulled away. I didn't particularly care what he could do for Williams, or the *Courier* either, but it would keep him out of trouble for a while. Some day I'd have to take him aside and tell him it was considered wrong to go around shooting at people, even with a .22. But this did not seem to be precisely the night for it. Maybe I wasn't precisely the man for it, either.

I headed out Wells Street, lurching on the streetcar tracks, toward Wendover Hills. The big boy had had an eventful night. He would need a drink in private. He would need to talk, in private. He would need company to share his triumph. He wasn't at Marge's place, so Marge must be at his. At least I hoped so. There wasn't too much time to make mistakes in. I kept remembering a girl who had spent four hours dying.

The streetcar tracks ended short of Wendover Hills, of course. People out there didn't need public transportation. I took the road as fast as I could, wishing I could drive like a jerk. You'd think a man who had nothing to live for wouldn't mind a little thing like passing blind on the curves. It occurred to me that I had been singing that dirge for quite a while now, but I never quite seemed to get around to blowing my brains out. There was something significant in that, I was sure, and I'd have to give it some thought, later. I made the turn and headed up through the private estates. There wasn't much time, so I just swung up the gravel drive when I got there, ducking low. They'd got the word and they were waiting. The windshield sprayed safety glass over my head and shoulders. I aimed the car at the source of the trouble, and hit a couple of things in the bushes before a tree stopped me. The doors popped open, which was convenient. Somebody was shooting from the other side of the drive.

I rolled a little ways and waited. He came running up, sure that I was dead. If he hadn't dodged the draft, he might have lived longer. The army would have taught him a few things. There's something very satisfying about the kick and bellow of a shotgun; it makes you feel you're accomplishing something. I moved away from there. They had the floodlights on at the house, now. I stopped to shake the splintered glass out of my hair and shirt. It was uncomfortable as hell. I shoved a fresh shell into the old 97. A pump gun is very handy in a fight; you can keep filling up the magazine without taking the gun out of action for a moment. I had never used one in a fight before—Uncle Sam doesn't issue them—but my theories on the subject were proving sound. Behind me, a guy began to scream for somebody to get the car off him. I let the hammer of the gun down to half-cock as I headed for the house. There was no sense in blundering around in the dark with a cocked gun. A man could stumble and shoot himself.

In a funny sort of way, it was just like hunting. Normally I'm a reasonably kindly sort of guy, I like to think, and if I meet up with a bird with a broken wing, out of season, I'll do as much as the next person to fix it up. Maybe a little more, because I like birds, and know them better than most people. But after the season opens, I have no sentimental qualms whatever about shooting them. That's what they're there for and that's what I'm there for. Well, the season was open out in Wendover Hills. A jerk came running across the lawn, drawn by the yelling behind me. He had a gun in his hand. I thumbed the hammer back, let him get past, aimed low, and cut his legs from under him. The hunting was good out in Wendover Hills. There are two people inside most of us. There's the guy you meet every day on the street; and then there's the guy you meet in the dark with a gun in his hand and cause to use it.

The only trouble with the shotgun was its distinctive voice. I left that place on my belly with a lot of stuff going over. It wasn't like the war. These boys were just popping away with pistols and hoping. They didn't know terrain and they didn't know night fighting. I made the fancy border of the veranda and wormed through the bushes while they ran around and yelled at each other. Brooks would have organized it but Brooks wasn't there. Brooks was busy elsewhere. Carl should have organized it, but Carl didn't. I had kind of thought he wouldn't. That left it up to the ersatz butler, who called a council of war in the driveway.

I put my back to the bricks of the house. The overhang of the veranda roof protected me from above. Somebody had been shooting from up there, earlier, and I thought I knew who it was, but he couldn't reach me now. He had never been as good a shot as he thought, anyway. I stepped up to the veranda and fired the sawed-off slantingly at the tiled floor. The ricocheting shot, twenty-seven pellets to the load, sprayed the three of them standing in the drive impartially. They thought they were killed. I fired again in the same place, and put another load at their heels as they ran.

Some day I would laugh at the memory of the picture they made, fleeing. Nothing was very funny at the moment. I fed the magazine again, and walked in the front door as if I owned the place. Nobody shot at me. There was a big hall and a big stairway and an upstairs hall kind of like a balcony. The door to the master bedroom was closed.

I said, "Carl, I'm coming in."

He did not answer.

I said, "If Marge is in there, and wants out, she's got ten seconds."

I counted to ten and nobody came out.

I said, "I've got a sawed-off twelve-gauge loaded with buck. You'd better make the first one good, because you won't get another."

I reached over and shoved the door open and jumped back. He fired twice. One bullet splintered the swinging door; the other hit somewhere inside the room; high, judging by the plaster that sifted down. That would be an accidental discharge as he tried to control the weapon. He liked the service .45, too; but it wasn't an easy gun to handle, particularly in rapid fire. It was always kind of like trying to work a pneumatic drill with one hand.

I said, "Load her up again, Carl. Here I come."

There was a straight, uncomfortable-looking chair standing against the wall. I picked it up and tossed it through the opening. He gave it one shot. I went in right behind it, hit on a shoulder, and kept rolling. He fired about three times, behind me every time. It was a big room and I used up most of it. Then I came to one knee and brought the shotgun up. A final bullet went past my ear. My finger was on the trigger but I didn't shoot. He was no use to me dead. He didn't shoot again, either. The room was full of plaster dust and the smell of smokeless powder. Marge was standing in a corner, not too scared. She was wearing a brassière and a tailored white skirt, somewhat wrinkled. The jacket that went with the skirt, unwrinkled, hung over the back of a chair. It occurred to me that the girl seemed to be fully and respectably dressed less than twenty-five percent of the time. There were drinks on the dresser. Champagne.

Carl said, "Don't think it isn't loaded just because I've fired seven. I had one in the chamber, and I shoved in a fresh clip after the first two."

I looked at him, and got to my feet very slowly, keeping the shotgun steady. "Does it matter, Carl?"

"What the hell are you trying to do, boy?" He laughed. "It's nothing to go Kamikaze about, is it? I did the best I could for you and the dame, but 't was no go. I never promised. . . . What do you want, anyway?"

I said, "Right now I want you to drop that gun. Let the hammer down first. No sense killing anybody by accident."

He laughed again. "You crazy, boy? Why should I do that? Maybe I haven't got quite as good a chance as you with that scattergun, but I'll take you with me."

"No," I said. "You won't."

"Tell me the reason."

"You know the reason," I said. "We both know the reason. Why weren't you down below when I came in, Carl?" His eyes wavered. I said, "Brooks is your gun, Carl. Brooks is your courage. But Brooks isn't here. He wasn't in another place we both remember." His face tightened. His hand tightened. On everything except the trigger. He couldn't manage that. I had kind of thought he wouldn't. He was a hell of a man, though. He looked like a house, standing there. He looked like a monument. I grinned at him. "Come on, big boy. I'm getting tired holding this thing. Either do it or get off the pot."

He tried again and almost made it. In a strange way, I almost wanted him to make it, even if I died for it. We had, after all, been through a lot together. Then his face went slack, and his thumb found the hammer and eased it down. It's not as simple as it looks, one-handed. You have to get the grip safety a certain way. But he knew the trick of it. Then he hurled the gun across the room and covered his face with his hands.

It took us fifteen minutes to track down Brooks by phone and give the orders. After Carl had said his piece, I took the instrument from him.

"This is Nyquist," I said. "I've got a shotgun in his back. If anything happens to the girl, I'll blow him in two."

There was silence at the other end of the wire; then the sound of the connection being broken. That left it up to Mr. Brooks. I did not let myself figure the chances. I walked across the room with the shotgun under my arm, and picked up Carl's pistol. It held three shells. I checked the action; but it takes more than being pitched against a wall to put that hand-cannon out of commission. I aimed at a spot on the wall-paper and pulled the trigger. Plaster flew within an inch or two of the place; she was sighted close enough. The trigger pull was lousy. Carl did not even flinch at the noise. Marge, who was putting on her jacket, looked up irritably, but did not speak. We went downstairs to wait.

The silence outside was tremendous. Guns had been fired and men had died and nobody gave a damn. You paid for privacy out here, and you got it. We could hear the big Lincoln coming blocks away. It swung into the drive, squeezed past the rear of my piled-up Plymouth without slacking speed, roared up to us, and skated to a halt in the light. Brooks was out of it almost before it had stopped, on the far side, holding the girl as a shield. She did not look too good; but she did not look too bad, either. At least she was alive. Brooks forced her around the front of the Lincoln, with her arm twisted up between her shoulder blades and his gun in her back.

"Fifty-fifty," Brooks said. "Carl goes; she goes."

I said, "I get more meat for my money." After a moment I said, "Last night you were brave as hell. Now you've got to hide behind a woman."

He said, "You've got too much gun against me."

"That can be fixed."

It was a stupid goddamn business. All we needed was a couple of horses and a ten-gallon hat apiece. I shucked the shell out of the shotgun and heaved the thing into the bushes and stepped clear. Carl did not move. He was a robot with the juice cut off. Marge had disappeared somewhere. That wasn't good, but there was nothing I could do about it. Brooks looked at me standing there, empty-handed, a pretty target, and temptation was strong inside him. But Hopalong Cassidy wouldn't have liked it. Roy Rogers would have slapped his wrist. The Lone Ranger would never have spoken to him again. He gave the kid a shove that sent her sprawling in the gravel—as safe a place as she could find under the circumstances—and pushed his gun into the holster.

"Any time," he said. "Any place."

"Now," I said, and we went into our act.

It was a simple enough problem: to get Carl's gun from my waistband, hit the safety with my thumb, raise the piece to eyelevel, and fire one aimed shot. I concentrated on making it good: there was no time to repair any mistakes. He fired by feel as his gun came clear, which was his funeral. The bullet cut my slacks at the knee. The tug threw me off slightly; I steadied down again, squeezed, and the pistol discharged.

The .45 automatic was developed after the old service .38 proved inadequate to cope with the Moros in the Philippines. If the .45 at close range has ever proved inadequate to cope with anything human, I haven't heard about it. The two-hundred-and-thirty-grain slug took Brooks in the chest and pushed him back a step. He tried to pull the trigger again, but the double-action mechanism of his revolver was suddenly too strong for him to work. He dropped the gun and fell on top of it. I suppose we had proved something. I waited until it was obvious that he was not going to move again.

Then there were headlights sweeping around the house. I helped the kid scramble to her feet. We sidestepped as Marge's Cadillac lurched up. Marge cried something urgent. Carl moved across the veranda like a zombie and got in, and the big car shot away, spraying gravel behind it.

I said, "You okay, kid?"

"Yes," she said. "Now."

I held her for a while. Presently we heard sirens. The neighbors had finally got around to calling the police. The kid giggled abruptly. I looked at her, thinking it was a little late for hysterics.

"That reporter," she said. "Williams."

"What about him?"

"He's lying in the back of that car all tied up like a mummy. I forgot all about him."

chapter twenty-nine

WE CAME out of police headquarters in broad daylight. Normally, I suppose, I would have been kept in jail until it could be decided which of my crimes to hang me for; but that morning the political climate was changing so rapidly in Capital City that nobody in the higher echelons was willing to stick his neck out by making a decision that might leave him vulnerable tomorrow. I was finally released more or less into the custody of the *Courier* as represented by Jack Williams.

The people on the street looked at the three of us oddly as we walked by, with some reason. What with first being beat up by Gunderman's boys and then playing Indian out in Wendover Hills, I was looking pretty disreputable; and Jack and Barbara had not come through the night in much better shape. We had been allowed washroom privileges—as well as coffee and stale doughnuts—by the police, but we still looked like charter members of the castaways' union. Fortunately, a colleague of Jack's had brought his pretty two-tone car around and parked it within a block of the place.

"Well, it was quite a night," Jack said, driving us away. "Quite a night and quite a story. We've got Maney on the run, now. Even if we can't hit him legally, we can laugh him out of public life. I just wish Arnold Brooks had lived to stand trial. Not that I'm criticizing, you understand, but I had the goods on that guy...."

He was quite happy, despite a few bruises and contusions. He hadn't had to kill anybody. Everything was working out swell for Jack Williams. Excitement had even cured him of a heartbreak that, I suspected, had been mostly imaginary, anyway. These crusaders are always looking for a Cause: something for which their hearts can bleed freely. Well, Jeanie had served her purpose, as far as Jack Williams was concerned; she was avenged and forgotten.

He switched on the radio as he drove, and listened to the six-thirty news broadcast that didn't say anything we didn't already know. I was interested to learn, however, that I was an outbreak of gang warfare unprecedented since the violent days of Chicago and Al Capone. Political revelations were promised but not made; somebody was still sitting desperately on the lid, but the pot was simmering.

"Wait till our extra hits the street!" Jack said. Our timing had been a little off; the *Courier* was normally an evening paper. He sounded like something out of *The Front Page*. The hell with Jack Williams. The boys with the typewriters and cameras serve a useful purpose, no doubt; but in the long run the decision is generally made by some rough character with a firearm. Or a club or a bow or a hydrogen bomb. Some day this might change, but it hadn't yet. I was feeling philosophical as hell. Lack of sleep always does that to me.

The kid sat silent between us. I was aware of her, and I suspected she was aware of me, but we had nothing to say that was for Jack Williams's ears. Presently she reached out to turn off the blatting radio. Jack grabbed her arm, as the announcer stopped talking about shampoo, and paused, and rustled some papers, and said in his best voice-of-doom manner:

"Folks, I've just been handed a shocking bulletin. I regret to have to tell you that Governor Maney, who was the victim of one vicious underworld attack only a week or so ago, was shot down this morning on the steps of the Executive Mansion by a small-time racketeer named Tony August. A withering hail of fire from the guns of three state troopers immediately cut the assassin down in his tracks, but too late to save the Governor's life. It is reliably reported that the motive for the crime was revenge for the death of August's brother, who was executed for a particularly revolting and brutal murder some months ago." The announcer drew a deep, sententious breath. "The whole state, regardless of party, will mourn the passing of Martin Maney, a great statesman and a martyr to the cause of good government."

He went back to extolling the merits of Sheen, the wonder shampoo. Jack Williams said a blasphemous word and switched off the radio.

"Well," he said, "there goes the story!"

The kid turned her head. "What do you mean?"

"Don't be silly," Jack said. "Three years from now, maybe

I'll write a sensational article debunking the late Martin Maney. Right now, no publisher would touch it with a ten foot pole. They're stopping the presses over at the *Courier* right now, and taking out everything but a nice respectful obituary. People don't like you to kick a dead politician—at least until he's been dead a decent interval. Hell, Maney's a martyr; didn't you hear the man?" Jack sighed. After a while, he asked, "Why would August blow his top like that? After all, he was willing to play along with this publicity stunt in the first place—"

I said, "Be your age, Jack. You don't think Tony was told it was a publicity stunt, do you? He played along because he thought I was shooting at Maney for keeps; and if he couldn't do the shooting himself he was happy to cover up for the guy who did. I missed my shot—the way he saw it—so I guess he just figured it was up to him to repair my mistake. Some of those jerks have pretty one-track minds."

"Oh," Jack said. Presently he said, "Something else I wanted to ask you. That visit of Maney's to the oculist—"

I said, "He had to have some reason for wearing sunglasses, didn't he; when he was known to consider any kind of glasses a menace to good eyesight? When a bullet hits there's bound to be some stuff flying around. Okay?"

"Well, it makes no difference now," Jack said resignedly. "But I knew there was something funny about that, just the same."

I thought it must be nice to be right all the time, like Jack Williams. He stopped the car at the light, got the green arrow, turned out Western, and pulled up in front of the shop. I got out. The kid got out beside me. We watched Jack drive off. Then we went upstairs. In the apartment, she walked across the living room to the mirror, pivoted to get the full effect, and laughed at her own appearance. She was really pretty grimy. Brooks had had her tied up in a cellar somewhere. She turned to face me.

"Well, I never did have much luck with this suit," she said, smiling at me. "The first time I wore it, a man made me crawl under a car."

"And the second time," I said, "you got married."

"I wasn't counting that as bad luck, Paul."

"Weren't you?"

Her smile had faded. She said quickly, as if to change

the subject: "Why didn't you tell me the truth, darling? Why did you let me think—"

"Think what?"

"That you were a cold-blooded murderer. Potentially, anyway. Why didn't you tell me it was just a . . . a publicity stunt? Why did you let me go to the police, Paul? All you had to do was tell me."

I shook my head. "No, you'd have gone anyway, sooner or later. Even if you could have stomached letting Tony take the rap for me—knowing it was all prearranged and Tony was willing—you'd sooner or later have felt it your duty to tell somebody the truth about Martin Maney, once you knew it. It was an impossible situation. The whole deal was impossible. I figured I might as well let nature take its course."

"Even if it killed you," she said quietly. "You were willing to die as long as I was safe. Weren't you?"

I grinned. "Cut it out, kid. I told you once I felt responsible for getting you into the mess. Man starts a job, he likes to finish it. . . . How do you feel?"

"Why, I feel fine," she said, and glanced down at her ruined clothes, and laughed. "Really, I'm all right, darling, even if I do look terrible. He hadn't got around to doing much except tell me what was in store for me, when the phone rang upstairs. I'm perfectly all right, Paul. Really."

I said, "Then you won't mind if I call up Pete Krumbein. He'll drive you to Grantsville. You can sleep in the back seat and be with your sister in time for dinner." Man starts a job, he likes to finish it. You can think all kinds of romantic and impractical thoughts in the middle of the night with death close by; but in the morning, safe and sleepy, you realize how farfetched they were. After all, I had come very close to wrecking the life of one girl not nearly as nice as this one. . . .

Slowly Barbara's face changed. "I see," she whispered.

"There's no point in dragging it out, is there?" I said. "That marriage license has served its purpose. As soon as things get straightened out a bit, I'll get in touch with somebody about the legal details." I turned to the phone. "Pete?" I said when the number answered. "Paul Nyquist here. Got a long haul for you. Start in half an hour. Can do?" I hung up. "He'll be here in half an hour."

She looked at me for a moment longer. Then she turned

on her heel and walked quickly into the bedroom and pulled the door closed behind her. It was some time before I heard the shower running. She did not come out again until the doorbell rang. When she did, I started forward to help her with her bag, but she seemed to be bearing up nicely under the weight, so I let it go. It was hardly the time for chivalry. There had already been too damn much chivalry, most of it phony. She was wearing navy-blue slacks and a jersey and looked a little like a boy, but not much. She stopped at the head of the stairs and looked back. I couldn't think of anything I particularly wanted to say; apparently she couldn't, either. She went on down the stairs. I heard the cab pull away.

I went into the bathroom and drew a tub of water, shed my clothes, climbed in, and entertained myself counting my scars and bruises, old and new. The game wasn't entertaining enough to keep me from thinking; so I climbed out, dried myself gingerly, and was contemplating what to wear when I heard somebody in the living room. It annoyed me that I couldn't help feeling a quick surge of elation. *What the hell did she have to come back for?* I asked myself. *Can't she see that it won't work?* But I wasn't kidding myself a bit. I found some moccasins and a dressing gown and went out there quickly.

Marge was sitting in the big chair. She was the only person in the room. It took me a moment to rearrange my thoughts to accept her presence.

"He killed himself," Marge said.

"What?"

"Carl," she said. "He took the gun I keep in the glove compartment. He put it in his mouth and pulled the trigger. I thought you'd like to know."

There was no expression on her face. She was wearing a dark dress and no jewelry whatsoever—mourning, I suppose. She looked almost plain.

"You killed him," she said. "Once you saved his life. Something happened that day, didn't it? There was always something between you. I don't want to know what it was. Today you killed him."

"Yes," I said.

She reached into her purse, and brought out a gun, and looked at it. There was some brown stuff dried into the checkering of the ivory grip.

"It's funny," she said. "I came here to shoot you."

It didn't seem to matter very much. "Go ahead," I said.

"Don't be silly," she said. "What the hell good would that do?" She put the gun away, rose, and brushed at her somber dress. "Well, so long, baby. It was nice knowing you. For a while, anyway."

After she had left, I walked over to the rack of guns on the wall. It wasn't half a bad idea, that one of Carl's, I reflected. We had neither of us been much good, either to ourselves or anybody else, since that day down in North Carolina. I took down the .45 automatic and looked at it. It was too much gun for the job; there was no sense in making that much of a mess for somebody to clean up. I put it back, and got the little target .22 instead. I took a loaded clip from the drawer, shoved it into place, and jacked a shell into place. Then I stuck the barrel into my mouth.

It seemed like an awkward shot to make; and I took it out and placed the muzzle against my temple. I felt remarkably silly, and knew that I couldn't pull the trigger if I stood there a million years.

"Who the hell are you trying to impress, anyway?" I said aloud, and unloaded the gun and put it back, and went out into the kitchen to make myself some breakfast. I had the bacon done and was cracking eggs into the grease in the skillet when I became aware of her standing in the doorway. After a while, I looked at her. She put the suitcase down.

"It seemed sort of stupid," she said. "Sort of stupid and pointless. Going, I mean. After all, I can always leave. It won't . . . it won't hurt any more five years from now than it does this morning. It can't. So we might as well try it. We may lose each other anyway, but it seems stupid not even to try. Or what do you think?"

I set the pan off the fire and went to meet her as she came across the room.